A shot rang out, hit[ting the] cruiser.

"Get down!" Jackson shouted and laid a hand across her back to push her down.

Rhea's heart thumped loudly as she struggled with her seat belt. Another shot sounded. She finally got her belt free and sank even lower, hoping the dashboard would provide cover.

Jackson had thrown his door open and knelt behind it for protection as he scoured the area. Another shot rang out, coming straight at them, and Jackson grabbed his radio.

"Shots fired. Aspen Ridge Road."

Another bullet pinged against the door by Rhea.

"Identify yourself," the dispatcher asked.

"Detective Whitaker. Regina PD. We're pinned down. Shots fired."

"Sending backup," the dispatcher said.

Jackson reached for his own weapon and shouted out to their assailant. "Police! Backup's on the way!"

The response was the roar of a car engine starting up and the squeal of tires...

Cold Case Reopened deals with topics some readers might find difficult, such as sexual assault and domestic violence. If you or someone you love is the subject of domestic violence, please consider contacting the National Domestic Violence Hotline at 1-800-799-7233.

COLD CASE REOPENED

New York Times Bestselling Author
CARIDAD PIÑEIRO

To my absolutely fabulous and amazing agent Michelle
Grajkowski. Thank you for believing in me. Thank you for being
such a beautiful person who can always bring a smile to my face
and make me laugh. May we share many, many more slices of
cheesecake together in the future!

HARLEQUIN®
INTRIGUE®

PLEASE RECYCLE

Recycling programs
for this product may
not exist in your area.

ISBN-13: 978-1-335-28454-9

Cold Case Reopened

Copyright © 2021 by Caridad Piñeiro Scordato

For questions and comments about the quality of this book,
please contact us at CustomerService@Harlequin.com.

Harlequin Enterprises ULC
22 Adelaide St. West, 40th Floor
Toronto, Ontario M5H 4E3, Canada
www.Harlequin.com

Printed in U.S.A.

New York Times and *USA TODAY* bestselling author **Caridad Piñeiro** is a Jersey girl who just wants to write and is the author of nearly fifty novels and novellas. She loves romance novels, superheroes, TV and cooking. For more information on Caridad and her dark, sexy romantic suspense and paranormal romances, please visit www.caridad.com.

Books by Caridad Piñeiro

Harlequin Intrigue

Cold Case Reopened

Visit the Author Profile page at Harlequin.com.

CAST OF CHARACTERS

Rhea Reilly—An artist who has done quite well for herself. She is a twin, and her sister is named Selene because their mother had a thing about Greek mythology.

Jackson (Jax) Whitaker—He served in Afghanistan as a marine before joining the Regina police force. He is in line to become police chief when the current chief retires.

Selene Reilly-Davis—Rhea's twin sister, who disappeared in Regina, Colorado. Her marriage was troubled and she was the victim of domestic abuse.

Matthew Davis—Selene's husband has a contracting business that is faltering. He seems charming to others, but has a violent temper.

Josefina (Sophie) and Robert (Robbie) Whitaker, Jr.— Jax's cousins who develop games and apps, as well as do ethical hacking. They often assist the Liberty Agency in Miami with their skills.

Mercedes Gonzalez—Married to Robert Whitaker, Jax's uncle, and works for the NSA as an analyst. Her family runs the Liberty Agency in Miami.

Robert Whitaker—Works for the NSA and occasionally with the Liberty Agency.

Chapter One

It was hard to believe that such beauty possibly held unspeakable evil.

Rhea Reilly stood on the shore of the mountain lake where six months earlier her twin sister, Selene, had disappeared on a cold fall night.

Rhea's artist's eye took in the scene before her. The waters of the lake sparkled like diamonds beneath a sunny cerulean sky. At the farthest end of the lake, the waters tumbled over a spillway for the dam that held back a rush of water during a spring thaw or heavy rain. In the distance, ragged mountains leaped into the sky, still frosted with the remnants of winter snow at the highest elevations.

Normally she would have savored painting such a lovely sight, but not today, when it might be her sister's watery tomb.

Rhea hugged her arms tight around herself, closed her eyes and listened to the soft lap of the water against the rocky shores of the lake. Imagined Selene standing there that fateful night, tapping out the message she'd sent to Rhea.

I can't take it anymore. I can't. I'm finally going to do something about it.

The police had taken that text to mean that Selene had decided to end her life that night, right there on the shores of those stunningly beautiful mountain waters. But Rhea wasn't convinced.

Although her sister had been troubled the last few months, Rhea was certain that Selene would never take her life. If anything, it was more likely that Selene's husband had killed her, but the police in Selene's hometown had been unable to find enough evidence to charge him. No-body homicides were apparently very difficult to prosecute.

The police here in Regina, Colorado, where Selene's car had been found by the lake, were convinced that her sister had committed suicide, even though they also hadn't been able to find Selene's body.

But Rhea was sure her sister wasn't dead. There was something inside her, that special twin connection they had always shared, that had been saying from the very beginning that Selene was alive and hurting.

That was why she'd undertaken her own investigation once her sister's case had become inactive because the police had run out of leads.

Rhea dashed away the tears that had leaked from beneath eyes screwed shut.

Her sister was alive and, if she wasn't, her husband was responsible. She intended for the police to do something about it based on the information she had collected over the last six months. But for the truth to come out, she needed more corroborating evidence and only the police could provide the resources to accomplish that.

She whirled, stumbled a bit on the rough rocks beneath her feet. Righting herself, she marched to her car, which she had parked on the street near where Selene's sedan had been found. The street would have been deserted when Selene had texted her that night.

Rhea stopped to look around, examining the scene. Along the edges of the lake, a marina spread out across the shore. Dozens of boats were parked at the docks behind a large building that held a restaurant, a marina office and a shop that sold supplies for boaters, as well as tourists, partaking in the lake's many summer activities.

Across the way were a few homes and in one of those homes was a witness who had seen Selene park and walk toward the lake. The older woman hadn't thought much of it because people often stopped, even at night, to take in the splendor of the lake.

Rhea intended to speak to her, but hopefully with the police to back her up and add their own expertise to the interrogation.

The police.

It all kept circling around to needing their assistance, so it was time she got going and spoke to them about Selene's case.

She got in her car and headed to Main Street and the Regina Police Station. As she cruised down Main Street, she was once again struck by the loveliness of the town. It was postcard-perfect, with its charming downtown filled with an eclectic mix of shops that catered to locals as well as the tourists who would visit for skiing and water sports.

Rhea found a spot just a block shy of the police station, parked and grabbed the thick folder bulging with the information she had gathered over the many months. With it tucked under her arm, cradled as securely as a newborn baby, she walked to the police station and paused at the base of the steps.

Like everything else about this town, the police station looked like something off a movie set. The building blended harmoniously with the other structures along Main Street. On either side of the wide steps leading to the door, spring flowers in a riot of colors cascaded over the edges of the terraced garden. Bright pink, purple and blue blossoms waved at her in welcome as a slight breeze swept across the street, still a bit cold despite it being early spring.

The chill settled in her bones as if warning her that she might not be happy with what she found inside.

She dragged in air through her nostrils and then expelled it with a harsh breath.

Time to get going. She stomped up the stairs and to the reception desk.

The sergeant at the desk did a little double take, as if seeing a ghost, and Rhea understood. She and Selene were identical twins and Selene's case had caused quite a stir in the normally placid town. It was unlikely that the police officer hadn't seen a photo of Selene in the station or on the news.

"I'm Rhea Reilly. Selene's sister. I was hoping to speak to the chief if he had a moment," she said. She hadn't made an appointment because she wasn't sure of the welcome she'd get. Especially considering how poorly the meeting with the Avalon police chief had gone. What with rumors about the Blue Code, she hadn't wanted to take any chances; the Regina police chief might not see her if word of her mission had traveled to him.

"I'll see if he's available," the officer said and gestured for her to take a seat in the reception area, but Rhea had too much nervous energy to sit. She paced as the young woman called the chief. Heard the murmurs as the officer spoke to him before rising to say, "The chief will see you, but he has only a few minutes before another meeting."

The young woman gestured toward the back of the building where the police chief stood at the door to his office. He was dressed in a bright blue shirt the color of the lake waters and dark blue pants. The shirt strained against a bull chest and broad midsection. A shiny gold badge pinned to the right breast of his shirt identified him as the chief while on the left breast the town's emblem was embroidered on a patch. White, blue and gold colors on the badge-shaped patch showed the mountains in the background, skiers on a slope to the left and a swimmer in waves to the right. *Tourists. The town's lifeblood*, Rhea thought. Because of that, a murder in their town was the last thing the police and town officials would want. Easier just to call it a suicide.

The chief did a "come here" wave with his hand, but his weathered face was set in stern lines, his mouth a harsh slash that was clearly at odds with his gesture.

Despite his less than friendly demeanor, she pushed through the barrier the desk sergeant buzzed open and marched to the chief's office, her folder tucked tight against her.

As she did so, she passed one man who sat handcuffed on a bench by an officer's desk.

Rough-looking with a heavily bearded face, he jumped, almost startled as she neared, and the color drained from his face. His hard eyes, dark and brooding, widened in surprise much like the desk sergeant's before he schooled the reaction.

Something about him sent a shiver of apprehension through her, but she tamped it down and proceeded to the chief's office.

"Miss Reilly," the chief said with a dip of his head and sweep of his hand to welcome her.

She sat in the chair across from him as he took a spot behind his desk. Like everything else about the town, the desktop and nearby bookcase were neat as a pin. So neat they almost looked staged, but then again, she remembered this chief being quite orderly and controlled. Compassionate even in the days after Selene's disappearance.

"What can I do for you today?" he said, as he laced his fingers together and leaned his thick forearms on the edge of his desk in a slightly friendlier posture.

The folder sat in her lap, heavy against her thighs. She shifted her hands across the smooth surface of it and said, "I really appreciate all that you've done for my family, Chief Robinson."

He dipped his head and his attitude softened a bit more. "Thank you. I know it was a difficult time for you. Rhea, right?"

She nodded. "Yes, Rhea. It was a difficult time and, again, I appreciate all that you did. What I'm hoping is that you'll reopen the case. I have new information—"

Chief Robinson held up his hands to stop her. "Miss Reilly, this isn't *Murder, She Wrote*. I'm sure you think you've unearthed some 'new evidence,'" he said, using air quotes for emphasis. "But we did a thorough investigation."

Anger built inside her at his dismissiveness, but she battled it back, certain it wouldn't help. "I know you did, but I've gotten more information—"

"Let me guess. From social media," he said with a rough laugh and wag of his buzz-cut head of salt-and-pepper hair.

She couldn't deny it. "Some of it. All I'm asking is that you let me show you what I've collected. Let me explain why I think…" She hesitated. The chief would never believe that Selene was still alive, but at a minimum she hoped that he would reopen the investigation and either find Selene or her killer.

At her silence, Chief Robinson leaned toward her again, compassion replacing his earlier disbelief. "Look, Miss Reilly. Rhea. I know this must still be difficult for you, but we have limited resources to…expend on this case."

She was certain he had really wanted to say "waste on this case" but she pressed on.

"Please, Chief Robinson. All I'm asking is that you look at this," she said and held up the bloated folder for him to see.

The chief stood. "I'm sorry. I have another meeting in a few minutes and have to prepare for it."

She'd been dismissed. Again, just like at the Avalon Police Department in her sister's hometown. But she didn't intend to give up.

"I'll be staying at the Regina Inn for a few days. Just in case you change your mind. And if not, rest assured I'll be reaching out to people in town to complete my investigation."

With that she shot out of her chair and escaped his office, her veiled threat hanging in the air. She was sure the chief would be less than pleased with her playing detective on his home turf. It would draw too much attention to the fact that not all was as perfect as it seemed.

She rushed through the pen of police officers and clerks, past the reception area and out the door, nearly running into an officer as he walked up the steps to the station.

"So sorry, miss," the officer said and caught her as she stumbled and dropped the folder. The rubber band around the folder snapped, and papers spilled out. She bent to collect them before the breeze swept them away.

DETECTIVE JACKSON WHITAKER kneeled to pick up the thick folder the young woman had dropped and round up loose papers. But, as he handed them to her and met her gaze, he felt gobsmacked.

Selene Davis. Her beautiful face was indelibly etched into his brain since he had been the one to find Selene's abandoned car by the lake.

Only Selene was dead, which meant this had to be her twin sister.

But before he could say anything, Selene's sister snatched the folder and papers from his hands and stomped off.

Whoa, so not happy, he thought and walked into the office, wondering what had set off the young woman. As he entered, he said to the desk sergeant, "That was—"

"Rhea Reilly. She wanted to speak to the chief," Desk Sergeant Millie Rodriguez answered and jerked her head in the direction of the chief's office.

Speaking of the chief, he stood at the door to his office, his features a picture of upset. His lips were set in a tight line, and his beefy arms crossed against his thick chest. With a sharp wave of his hand, the chief summoned Jackson to come over.

Certain that he knew just what this meeting would be about, Jackson hurried to the chief's office but didn't take a seat. He stood before the desk, hands jammed into his pockets, rocking back and forth on his heels as he waited for the older man to sit. Once he had, the chief looked up at him and said, "That was Rhea Reilly."

Jackson nodded. "I gathered as much. She's a

dead ringer for her sister. Twins if I remember correctly."

"You do. Rhea has been doing her own investigating and wants us to reopen her sister's case," Chief Robinson said and laid his muscled forearms on the edge of his desk.

Jackson considered the request, but only for a second. "It's hard for people to accept that someone they knew and loved would kill themselves. I imagine it's even harder for a twin."

The chief's eyebrows drew together in puzzlement, creating a deep furrow across his broad forehead, and Jackson quickly explained, "That twin connection some people claim they have."

"You believe that?" the chief asked, leaned back in his chair and steepled his fingers before his lips, scrutinizing Jackson as if he was a bug under a microscope.

Considering what he had seen of Selene's sister and her anger, she clearly believed something contrary to what their report had said. Because of that, Jackson shrugged. "Stranger things have been known to happen."

The chief continued to stare at him, as if sizing him up. "You know you're my choice to replace me when I retire next year."

Jackson nodded. "I do, and I appreciate your confidence in me. I promise that you'll be leaving the department in good hands."

"I think so. Maybe it's time I turn over some

of the more difficult tasks to you, so that you acclimate to that position."

Jackson wasn't above hard work. His years in the military and on the police force had been filled with long days. Tough days, like the day he'd finally had to close Selene's case as a suicide. It had bothered him then because, much like Rhea, it had been hard for him to understand how a beautiful and vibrant woman with so much to live for could just walk into the lake and end her life.

"Whatever you need me to do, Chief," he said with a dip of his head to confirm his acceptance of any task his boss assigned to him.

"I want you to look at Rhea Reilly's information and then tell her she's barking up the wrong tree."

Chapter Two

Rhea had barely finished unpacking her things when the knock came at the door.

She hurried there and threw it open, expecting to find room service with the extra blanket she'd requested. That earlier chill hadn't left her, not that a blanket would end it, but it had been worth a try.

It wasn't room service. It was six-plus feet of lethal male, dressed in police blues, with a white Stetson held in hands that he shifted uneasily on the brim. He had shortly cropped sandy-brown hair that screamed former military and eyes the gray of lake waters on a dreary day. He clenched and unclenched his chiseled jaw as he stood there, obviously hesitant, before he finally said, "You should be more careful and check to see who it is before you open the door."

Anger ignited instantly at his chastisement. "I was expecting room service. Not the police."

He tipped his head, seemingly sorry, but he didn't strike her as the type to apologize. Not willingly anyway. And it occurred to her then that he was the officer she'd run into outside the police station. The one who'd helped her pick up her papers and whom she hadn't thanked.

"Rhea Reilly," she said and held out her hand. "I'm sorry I was so rude before. I was upset."

"I understand. Detective Jackson Whitaker. Jax to my friends." A ghost of a smile danced across full lips, and he enveloped her hand with his big calloused one.

His touch roused a mix of emotions. Surprising comfort. Unwelcome electricity and heat.

"We're not friends…yet," she said as he continued holding her hand, longer than expected. Longer than necessary. She withdrew her hand from his and wrapped her arms around herself. "And I doubt that you can possibly understand."

That slight dip of his head came again, as if accepting her statement, and he motioned inside her room with his Stetson. "Do you mind if I come in?"

She both did and didn't mind. Something about his presence was unnerving, but if he was here, maybe it meant that the chief had reconsidered her request.

"Please," she said and waved him in.

He entered and, as he did so, his gaze swept the room, assessing. Observant. A cop's eyes taking in the scene and immediately focusing on the thick folder sitting on a small bistro table beside

French doors to a balcony facing the lake. The lake was a constant reminder of why she was here.

"May I?" he said and pointed toward the folder.

"Is that why you're here? Did Chief Robinson change his mind?"

JAX HATED TO burst her bubble so quickly, but he also didn't believe in lying. "The chief asked that I review your information."

Rhea narrowed her eyes, a bright almost electric blue that popped against creamy-white skin and dark, almost seal-black hair. "He just wants to shut me up, doesn't he?"

"Whatever he may want, I promise you that I'll be objective when I look at your information," he said and meant it.

Rhea focused her eyes even more pointedly and then suddenly popped them open, as if surprised. "Detective Whitaker. You were the officer who found Selene's car."

He nodded. "I was. I also secured the scene and took part in the investigation afterward."

"And you agreed with the conclusion that Selene killed herself," Rhea pressed and laced her fingers together before her. An assortment of silver and gold rings decorated her slender fingers while a mix of bracelets danced on her delicate wrist.

With a quick, negligent lift of his shoulders,

he said, "The evidence we had available indicated that, Rhea. I know that's a hard thing to accept—"

"Selene would not do that. She was too full of life to just throw it away," she said and shook her head, sending the shoulder-length locks of that dark hair shifting against the fine line of her jaw.

Jackson couldn't argue that it had seemed unlikely at first to him, as well. That her disappearance was likely foul play at her home prompted him to ask, "Why didn't you go to the Avalon police with your information?"

Rhea looked away and worried her lower lip and in that instant he knew. "You went to them and they didn't believe you, did they?"

She shook her head again, a softer almost defeated motion, and as she glanced his way, her gaze held the sheen of tears. Damn, but he couldn't handle tears. They were his kryptonite. He held his hands up and said, "I'm sorry, Rhea. But you have to understand that we're both small towns with limited resources."

"And what's one missing woman, right? Do you have any idea how many women go missing every year? How many women deal with domestic abuse every day? End up dead because no one believes them?" she said, her voice husky with suppressed tears and anger.

He nodded and juggled his Stetson in his hands. "I do. My sister…" He hesitated, the reality all too real for him still. "She was lucky. She got out."

"I'm sorry, Detective," she said and walked over to stand hardly a foot from him. She was so close he could smell her fragrance, something flowery and clean, like the scent of a spring day. The top of her head barely came to his chin. She was fine-boned beneath the gauzy floral fabric of her blouse. So slight, and he imagined Selene must have been built much the same. It bothered him to think any man would beat on her.

"We had no indication of domestic abuse when we investigated," he said as Rhea removed some papers from her folder and laid them out for him on the smooth mahogany table.

With a shrug of her slight shoulders, she said, "She never told me, but I had sometimes seen bruises on her arms. She always had an excuse for them. After she…disappeared, I found out that Selene had gone to a domestic violence support group. Just once. Only once…"

Her voice trailed off, and she fixed her gaze on the papers, avoiding his.

Jackson placed his thumb under her chin and applied gentle pressure to urge her to face him. "It's hard for people to admit they're being abused."

"And it's even harder to admit that someone you love killed themselves," she shot back, clearly anticipating what he would say, but Jackson didn't want to fight with her right now. You had to pick your battles, and he intended to save his ammunition for what would happen after he looked at her evidence. For when he might have to tell her that she was "barking up the wrong tree."

"May I take this information? Take a look at it?" he asked, intending to review the materials later that night after he had finished his shift.

Rhea hesitated, almost like she'd be trusting a stranger with her only child. It bothered him, but he tried not to show it. "I'm the one shot you have to reopen this case, Rhea. You've got to trust that I'll look at this objectively."

She laughed harshly and twisted away from him. Her loose blouse swirled around her slim midsection and then she faced him again with a heavy sigh. "I bet the chief told you to bury this. Am I right about that, Jax?" she said, emphasizing his name in a way that said they were anything but friends.

Since he believed honesty was the best policy, he said, "He did, but I'm not the chief. If I give you my word that I'll look at this with an open mind, you can bank your money on it."

"The Code of the West? Or the Blue Code? Which will it be?" she challenged, one dark brow flying up like a crow taking wing.

Exasperated, he blew out a heavy sigh and jammed his hat on his head. "I gave you my word. So what will it be?"

She settled her gaze on him, assessing him again. Then in a flurry of motion, she gathered all the papers and stuffed them into the folder. Grabbed it and handed it to him. "Don't disappoint me, Detective."

He cradled the binder to his side like a fullback cradling a football, put a finger to the brim of his Stetson and nodded. "Like I said, I give you my word."

He pivoted on his cowboy-booted heel and marched out of the room, intending to make good on his promise no matter what the chief had said.

The little voice in his head pestered him with, *What will you do if Rhea is right?*

I'll fight that battle when I get to it, he responded.

RHEA WAS TOO wired to finish unpacking after the detective's visit. So she did the one thing she always did when she needed peace. She drew.

She grabbed her knapsack, which always held a sketch pad, pencils, erasers and a blanket she could spread out to make herself comfortable while she worked. She snatched a jacket against the spring breeze, slung her knapsack over her shoulders and hurried out of the inn and onto Main Street.

The inn was at the farthest end of the street, away from the nearby highway that ran all the way from where her sister lived in Avalon to Denver, where Rhea had her home and art gallery. Her pace was hurried at first since she was in a rush to sketch, but there was a peacefulness about the town that was impossible to ignore. It seeped into her body, replacing the earlier chill she'd experienced. Slowing her headlong flight, she took the time to window-shop, appreciating the eclectic mix of shops.

By the time she reached the end of Main Street, her itchiness to draw because she was upset had been replaced by a desire to capture the charm of the quaint town nestled beneath a cloudless sky and the jagged snow-frosted peaks of the mountains in the distance.

A low stone wall with a wide granite ledge ran across the end of the block, marking the entrance to downtown. She opened her knapsack, pulled out the blanket and her materials and began to sketch. With swift determined strokes, an image of the town took shape on the paper. The trim and neat shops with their wooden signs and shiny windows. The many pots of flowers and shrubs before the shops. The wooden posts with street-lights that looked like old-time gas lanterns.

Beyond that, the slopes leading up to the nearby mountains, thick with evergreens in shades ranging from deep green to the bluish-gray of the spruces. Here and there big clumps of spring green identified groves of aspen that in the fall would turn golden, making for a spectacular display against the darker evergreens.

It popped into her brain that dozens, sometimes even hundreds, of aspens were often joined underground by a single root network, making them a massive living organism.

It made her wonder if the loss of one of those intertwined trees caused pain to the others. If they felt the connection the way she did with Selene. A connection that hadn't diminished despite Selene's disappearance. It was the reason she believed with all her heart that her sister was still alive, not that she would tell the detective that. He would dismiss it without question, so she had kept it secret to avoid dissuading him from reopening the case.

But she knew that eventually she would have to tell him, because if they couldn't confirm that Selene's husband, Matt, had killed her or that Selene had killed herself…

She shut her sketch pad abruptly. She'd finish the sketch later, when her mind wasn't as distracted. Packing everything away, she put on her knapsack and marched to the side of the street she hadn't visited yet.

Little by little peace filtered in, but it was tempered by the reality that her sister's last steps might have been down these streets. That these were the last images she might have seen.

Or that maybe they were the images she still saw if she was alive.

As she neared the spot opposite the inn where she was staying, she paused and turned, feeling as if someone had been following her. But there wasn't anyone there who seemed to have any interest in her. Shoppers went from store to store, or just strolled up and down the quaint downtown streets.

She rolled her shoulders, driving away the uneasiness, and did a quick look around to once again confirm she was just imagining the sensation. Satisfied, she returned to the inn to drop off her knapsack and relax before going in search of dinner.

Not that she could really relax with Detective Whitaker's decision hanging over her head. A decision that would make all the difference to her sister's case and maybe even help find Selene if she was still alive.

She hung on to that thought and the hope that Detective Whitaker would keep his promise. That he would keep an open mind to look at the evidence she had diligently gathered over the last six months.

An open mind that would help her find her missing sister.

Chapter Three

It had been a tiring day, filled with the kinds of routine things Jackson had come to expect in Regina.

A fender bender when someone had pulled out of a parking spot without looking.

A couple of tickets for speeding or running a red light. Another for someone failing to leash their dog in one of the public parks.

At a pub located close to the highway, which sometimes hosted a rougher crowd, he had been forced to issue a warning about a minor public disturbance.

Mundane things. Some might even say boring, but Jackson relished it after the many years he'd spent in the military. He'd seen too much death and destruction in Afghanistan, which was why he'd turned down jobs in other areas for the peace and tranquility of his hometown of Regina.

Selene's disappearance six months earlier had upset that serenity. From the moment the BOLO had come in and Jackson had discovered her car by the lake, it had been days of nonstop action. Securing and scrutinizing a possible crime scene. Coordinating with the Avalon Police Department and, after, searching the lake for Selene's body. A body that had never been found and maybe never would be if the spillway had been open, allowing her body to go over the dam and down the river.

It had taken a few weeks for things to die down. For the press to stop pestering the police and people in town about Selene's disappearance.

Things had gone back to normal, but now Rhea was here and determined to ask questions, possibly upsetting that peace.

But Jackson had never refused any mission in the military, no matter how scary or dangerous. He'd led his team on assignment after assignment and was proud to say he'd kept them safe with a level head and preparation.

He would do that with Rhea's request.

Much like he had prepared for a mission, knowing all he could about the terrain and the enemy, he intended to do the same with Rhea and find out more about her.

He put up a fresh pot of coffee, poured himself a big mug and sat down at his hand-hewn cedar kitchen table. Grabbing his laptop, he logged on to his police department account and searched through their resources for any information on Rhea Reilly. No criminal record of any kind. Not even a speeding ticket.

Hitting that dead end, he shifted his focus to a search of public information on the internet and quickly had hundreds of hits. Rhea Reilly was apparently a critically acclaimed artist who worked in several different disciplines. Oils, watercolors and mixed media. She owned the building where she lived and had a number of tenants who rented apartments, and a shop, from her.

The building was located on the 16th Street mall in Denver, a popular location for both locals and tourists. She also had an art gallery at the location, and he surfed to the gallery's website. From the portfolio on the site, it was clear that Rhea sold not only her work, but that of local artists, and not just paintings. Photographs, jewelry, pottery and other art pieces were proudly displayed on the site.

He scrolled through the images but was pulled back to Rhea's work time and time again. He understood why Rhea was so successful. There was so much…life in her work. Passion. The images jumped off the screen with their vibrancy, much like the woman he had met earlier that day.

Filled with life. Filled with passion for finding out what had happened to her sister. Stubborn, too. He had to throw that one in, as well, and he suspected that she wouldn't back down even if he refused to reopen the case.

The case, he thought as he set aside his laptop and pulled over the bulging folder with Rhea's evidence.

Opening it, he found it as neat and organized as any case file he'd ever prepared. The pages held timelines of Selene's husband's possible movements from Avalon to Regina and back, and then up to his client's building location in the mountains just outside Avalon.

The timelines she had documented, if true, deviated from the account Selene's husband, Matt, had provided in the days after his wife's disappearance.

Matt's testimony about the bonfire in his backyard was also contradicted by Rhea's evidence. According to the neighbors she had spoken to, Matt had kept the bonfire going almost overnight and not just for a short time to dispose of some leaves and branches.

Had he done it to dispose of Selene's body? Jackson wondered. *Was it even possible to cremate someone so completely in a home bonfire?*

Rhea had also reviewed the state of Matt's SUV the morning after Selene's disappearance. She had combined photos of his newly detailed SUV with those of his client's building location and the road leading to it, graveled and in relatively good condition. Not a dirt road that would have muddied his SUV, as Matt had claimed.

Not to mention the nighttime trip to a building location. It had hit him as implausible when he had heard that detail from the Avalon police, but they had investigated and found that the alibi held water.

But as Jackson went through all of Rhea's detailed notes, photos, maps and more, it was impossible for him to ignore the discrepancies that were piling up, deeper and deeper, like the winter snows when they came.

He leaned back in his chair, cradled the now almost-empty coffee cup and scrutinized the materials. Sucking in a breath, he shot to his feet and poured himself another cup. He searched through the junk drawer for a pen and pad and sat down once again, taking notes as he went through the papers a second time. He added his own questions to those that Rhea had raised until he had filled a few pages in his pad.

An ache blossomed in his back, and he tossed his pen onto the paper. He rose slowly, unfolding his large frame vertebrae by vertebrae into a stretch until the ache died down. Pacing around his kitchen, he ran his hand through his hair as he considered all the questions jumping around in his brain. Once the ache had been relieved, he returned to the table, leaned his hands on the top rung of the chair and examined all the materials again. Stared at his own pad of growing notes and questions.

With a sharp shift of his shoulders and a jagged exhale, he realized that there was only one thing he could do.

THE HAMBURGER SHE'D eaten hours earlier sat heavily in her stomach, keeping her awake.

It had been a large burger and quite tasty. Since she hadn't eaten all day, she'd scarfed down the burger and fries, but was paying the price for it now.

She was about to give up on sleep when the thump against the French door frame drew her attention.

Is someone trying to open it? she thought and held her breath, listening intently for any other sounds.

A rattle and another slight thump came again, louder. As if someone was jerking the door handle, trying to enter.

Her heartbeat raced in her chest as she carefully reached for the smartphone beside her bed, telling herself she was mistaken about what she was hearing. But the rattle came again and was followed by a scratching sound against the frame of the door.

She had no doubt now that someone was trying to break into her room.

She leaped from the bed, her phone in her hand and held it up, shouting as she did so.

"I'm calling 911! You hear me! I'm calling 911!" she shouted, while also engaging the camera and snapping off a burst of shots of the French door, hoping to capture an image of whoever was on the other side of the glass. For good measure, she raced toward the fireplace and grabbed a poker from the andirons. She held it up and said, "I'm armed! I'll use this!"

Heavy footsteps pounded across the balcony and down the fire escape, confirming that she hadn't been wrong. Someone had been out there.

Her own heart pounding as loudly as the footsteps, she raced back to the night table and snapped on the light. She pulled out Detective Whitaker's business card and dialed his number, hands shaking as she did so.

He answered immediately, almost as if he had already been awake. "Detective Whitaker."

"It's Rhea. Someone just tried to break into my room."

JACKSON RACED OVER to the Regina Inn, where a police car sat in front, watching the building.

He pulled up behind the cruiser, got out and approached the officer behind the wheel.

"Good evening, Officer Daly. Have you seen anything since I called?" he said.

The young man shook his head. "Nothing except the innkeeper coming out to ask what was happening. She's upset that someone might have tried to break in, but also that we're drawing too much attention."

Jackson understood. "Do me a favor and pull around the corner where you're not as visible. That might help if someone was here and decides to come back. They won't spot you on the side street."

He pulled his flashlight from his belt and walked the grounds around the inn. At the fire escape there were clear signs of footprints on ground softened by yesterday's rain.

To avoid any further upset, he dialed Rhea to advise her that he was coming up and also dialed the innkeeper.

The innkeeper met him at the door in a bathrobe she had tossed on, her face filled with worry. Lines of tension bracketed her mouth and her hair was in disarray, as if she had repeatedly run her fingers through it.

"Mrs. Avery. I'm so sorry to drag you out of bed at this late hour," he said with a tip of his head and swept his Stetson off as he entered.

"Is everything okay? Do we need to worry?" she asked, clutching the lapels of her robe with age-spotted hands.

He hated to cause upset but had no choice. "There's evidence someone was in the area of the fire escape. I need to check Rhea's room and balcony just to confirm and will let you know once I finish my investigation."

"Investigation?" she hissed and glanced up the stairs to the guest rooms.

"If something happened, I don't think you have to worry about the other guests, and we'll try to keep things quiet," he said, understanding the older woman's concern.

Jackson went up the stairs, careful not to make noise so as to not wake the other guests. He tapped softly on her door, and it flew open.

Like the innkeeper, Rhea had a robe wrapped tightly around herself, dark hair tousled. Her face was pale and she worried her lower lip for a second before she said, "Thank you for coming so late at night."

"Just doing my job," he said, although he had already started thinking of Rhea as something other than just a job. "May I check the door?"

She nodded, and he hurried over. He opened the French door and looked out. Muddy areas on the balcony appeared to be footprints. He slipped onto the balcony, avoiding the footprints, and noted that some paint had been scratched off the frame close to the latching mechanism. Someone had clearly been trying to pry it open.

He slipped back in, closed the French door and locked it shut. For good measure, he engaged the security bolts at the edges of both doors that would prevent it from sliding open even if someone broke the lock.

When he faced her, she stood hugging herself, obviously fearful. "Please tell me I was imagining it."

He shook his head. "You weren't. Someone

tried to get in. When you called you said you snapped off some photos. May I see them?"

She nodded, slipped her hand into the pocket of the robe and removed her smartphone. She unlocked it and handed it to him.

The blurry shots of the doors didn't show much. If you looked closely, there was a shadow on the balcony, but the photos were too dark to reveal much about whoever had been out there.

He handed her the phone. "I'm sorry. There's not much to work with, but someone was there. Did the person look familiar?"

She quickly shook her head. "I couldn't see much. I was too scared. I'm sorry."

Jackson walked over and laid a comforting hand on her forearm. "No need to apologize, Rhea. You were understandably frightened. If you had to guess who—"

"Matt. Selene's husband. He's angry that I'm pushing for Selene's case to be reopened," she immediately said.

Her response was possibly a little too quick. "How do you know?"

She swiped her screen again and held it up for Jackson to read Matt's message.

I've had enough of your lies and the trouble you're making for me. Leave me alone.

"You think he knows that you want to reopen the case?" Jackson asked.

Her answer came quickly again. "Yes. I think he has a connection on the force. Someone who works for Matt when he's not on duty."

Since it wasn't unusual for officers to have second jobs for when they had multiple days off on their shift, it didn't seem unlikely that there was some overlap between the police force and a local contractor. But it was something he'd have to check out, if his chief agreed to let him proceed with the investigation.

"I'll speak to the Avalon Police Department and have them see if Matt's at home. In the meantime, I can stay—"

"I'm okay. There's no need for you to stay," Rhea said, thinking that while the detective's presence would be comforting in one way, it would be disturbing in another. He called to her too strongly in a physical way. Even with tonight's upset, he was hard to ignore.

Jackson narrowed his gaze, considering her, but then he heaved his shoulders up in a shrug. "If you're sure, but I'll arrange for an officer to stay outside and keep an eye until the morning."

Only until the morning, Rhea thought. "What happens after that?"

Jackson hesitated, but finally said, "After that, we'll decide what to do."

"With an open mind?" she reminded him, still

worried about what he thought about the evidence she had gathered.

"With an open mind," he confirmed and then gestured to her front door. "I have to get going. If you need anything, don't hesitate to call."

She dragged a hand through her hair and blew out a harsh breath. "I won't. Thank you for coming tonight."

He tipped his head. "Just doing my job, Rhea."

But as his gaze met hers, Rhea suspected that he was thinking of her as more than just a job. Her heart sped up at the thought, but she tamped it down.

Her one-and-only involvement with the handsome detective had to be finding out the truth about Selene's disappearance.

Anything else was out of the question.

Chapter Four

"You want to do what?" Chief Robinson said, eyes wide in disbelief.

"I want to reopen the Selene Davis case, Chief." He sat in front of the older man's desk, leaned toward him and argued his case before his boss totally shut him down.

"I looked at all the materials Rhea gathered."

"It's Rhea now, is it?" the chief muttered.

"It is because I was trying to establish a rapport with her in order to determine if she was a crackpot or genuine," he said and plowed on. "She's genuine, Bill."

His chief sniggered and shook his head. "Never figured you'd let a pretty face sway you."

The heat of anger burned through his gut, but he tempered the flame. "If that's what you really believe, then maybe I shouldn't be your choice for police chief when you retire."

His boss's big body shuddered with a rough laugh and he wagged his head again. "I'm sorry, Jax. You know I trust you—"

"Then trust me on this, Bill. I looked through all her materials. Did a thorough review just like you asked. There are major discrepancies in Selene's husband's alibi and his actions the night she disappeared. And neither us nor the Avalon Police Department were aware of the fact that there might have been domestic violence going on," he said, arguing his case the way a lawyer might before a jury.

Chief Robinson laced his fingers together and placed his hands behind his head. He leaned back and his chair creaked from his weight. "I know that's a hot-button topic with you on account of Sara."

"It is, but you have to admit that if we'd had that info we would have looked at Matt Davis much more closely since—"

"Most murdered women have previously been victims of domestic violence," his chief finished for him.

With a chop of his hand against his palm for each item, he said, "There's evidence he abused her. His business was in trouble. The life insurance payout would keep that business afloat. He had a bonfire going almost all night. Who keeps a bonfire unattended for that long and takes a trip up a mountain at night to look at a building site?"

The chief swung back toward his desk and laid his forearms on the edge, steepled hands held before him. "What about a body, Jax? Hard to charge someone without a body."

With a dip of his head, Jackson agreed. "True, but we didn't find a body in the lake and were still prepared to label it a suicide."

When his boss didn't respond, he forged ahead. "I know it's all circumstantial, but we may be able to make a case. Maybe that's why someone tried to break into Rhea's room last night. Either to silence her or to get their hands on the evidence she collected."

Chief Robinson scrubbed his face with his hands. "This could be embarrassing for both departments, Jax. And if it is, you can forget ever becoming police chief here or anywhere for that matter."

"I know that, Bill. But again, none of us were aware of the abuse. If we had known we would have handled the investigations differently."

With a sweep of his hand, the older man said, "Go ahead, Jax. But if this all goes south—"

"I'll take responsibility for it, Bill. Count on that. I won't dishonor the department no matter what."

RHEA HADN'T BEEN able to sleep after what had happened. She'd snapped on the television and snuggled on a couch with a clear view of the French doors and windows, the heavy brass poker resting by her side. In the early morning hours she'd dozed off, but woke as the sun rose and bathed her room with light.

She'd made a cup of coffee and sat impatiently, waiting for the detective's call, even if only to arrange for the return of her folder. She was surprised when he suggested that they meet for lunch to discuss her materials and last night's intruder.

She tried to tell herself not to be too optimistic. Not to believe that the detective might actually be reopening her sister's case. She didn't want to have her hopes dashed, as they had been when she'd gone to the Avalon Police Department.

But then again, that police department hadn't even taken a moment to review her evidence. The Regina Police Department had.

Or at least she hoped the detective had done as promised.

At the restaurant, Detective Whitaker had already taken a seat at a table by a window. As she entered and met him, he straightened his long, lean form and wagged his head in greeting.

"Miss Reilly."

"Detective Whitaker. Thank you for meeting with me, and thank you again for last night."

"I wish I could say it's my pleasure, but we both know this meeting isn't about pleasure." He pulled out a chair for her.

She sat and clutched her hands together tightly in her lap. "Have you made a decision?"

A momentary flicker of some emotion, indecision maybe, flashed across his face. "I have, but first, I'd like to know more about Selene. About you."

It was her turn to hesitate. With a quick shrug, she said, "We were very close as you can imagine. Inseparable until Selene got married."

"What happened then?" He angled his big body toward her as if to hear her better. His gray gaze, steely with determination, fixed on her face. Slightly unnerving professionally and personally. Her body responded to him in a way it never had to any other man, maybe because she wasn't used to being around such physically powerful and lethally potent men.

She shifted her chair back a little. "We grew up in Boulder but moved to Denver for school. Roomed together during college and after. My career took off like a rocket while Selene was getting her master's."

"She was a teacher?"

"She's a music teacher, but also a very talented pianist and singer. She often performs in Denver when she visits," she said and her voice grew husky with emotion.

He stroked a hand down her arm to offer comfort. "Take your time, Rhea."

She nodded, dragged in a breath and released it with a rush of words. "She got a teaching job in Avalon and moved there. Met Matt and they married. After that we would have regular girls' weekends, mostly in Denver. Matt didn't like having me around."

"Maybe because you saw more than you should," Jackson said, sympathy alive in his tone.

With a shrug, she continued. "Maybe. When I first saw the bruises, I asked Selene how she'd gotten them. She told me she had fallen while on a hike. I forced myself to believe it, but then it happened again. A few times, but Selene had an excuse each and every time."

"You can't blame yourself, Rhea."

"But I do. I tell myself that if Selene's dead…" She stopped short, well aware of the slip and that the detective had caught it. For a long moment she sat there, trying to decide whether to be honest, but if she was anything, she was honest.

"Something was off that night after the text. I knew Selene was in trouble. I still feel her—" she tapped her chest "—in here. I know she's still alive."

Long moments passed, but as she peered at the detective's face, she had no clue what he was thinking. His face was as stern and stony as the summits of the mountains in the distance.

The waitress approached at that moment, but sensing the tension between them, and at Jackson's raised hand, she walked away.

As he had before, the detective leaned toward her and, in a low voice, he said, "Selene is gone, Rhea. We both wish it was different—"

"She's alive. I know it," she insisted, and his features softened as he sat back. She worried that she'd blown whatever chance she had of his reopening the case. But then he said, "Promise me one thing, Rhea."

Relief speared through her. "Whatever you want."

He arched a brow. "I know you're not normally that agreeable. If you were, we wouldn't be sitting here discussing this."

She couldn't argue with him. When it came to finding out what happened to her sister, she'd fight him tooth and nail if she had to. "You're right. What is it you want so that you'll reopen the case?"

"Promise me that you'll accept Selene's gone if that's what all the evidence says."

Accept that her sister was gone. Forever. That they'd never have another girls' weekend. Never share another laugh. Or cry. Never see that face that was like looking in a mirror. Something that anyone who wasn't a twin could never understand.

"That's some promise," she said and swiped away the tears that spilled down her cheeks.

The detective looked away and muttered something under his breath. *Kryptonite*, she thought he said before locking his gaze on her again. "Well? Rhea?"

"I promise."

JACKSON SUCKED IN a deep breath, held it and in a rush said, "I spoke to the chief, and we're reopening the case. Especially after last night."

Rhea's face paled, and she leaned away from the table. "It was Matt, wasn't it?"

He looked away for a moment, but then focused his gaze on her. "The Avalon police went by his house. It doesn't seem as if he was home."

"And if he wasn't, he was here," she said as she dragged a hand through her hair, making the thick locks dance around her face.

"Possibly. It's something I'll have to investigate."

She gestured between the two of them. "We'll investigate. I want to be a part of this investigation."

Jackson shook his head vehemently. "No way, Rhea. This is a police investigation."

Rhea shifted toward him, the blue of her eyes icy cold. "There wouldn't even be an investigation without me." She tapped a finger to her chest. "*I'm* the one who got all this evidence. *I'm* the one who knows the information inside and out."

"And *you're* the one who is too close to this. Too close because it's your twin, your mirror image. The person who is a part of your soul," he shot back.

A pregnant silence hung in the air, heavy with emotion, but then Rhea broke that silence

in words barely above a whisper, as her gaze
sheened with tears yet again.

"You made me a promise and you kept it," she
said, voice husky with feeling.

He nodded. "I did."

"I made you a promise, as well. But the only
way I can keep it, that I can know Selene is gone,
is if you let me be a part of this investigation."

Silence reigned again as Jackson considered
her request. As he skipped his gaze over her features, taking in her pain and her determination.
She wouldn't rest until she had an answer. And
she would never believe that answer unless she
was certain that he had turned over every stone,
even the tiniest pebble. Because of that, there was
only one thing he could think to say.

Chapter Five

"Okay."

She jumped, startled by that one-word answer. "You mean that? You'll let me help you?"

He nodded. "I hope I don't live to regret this, Rhea."

"You won't, Detective. You won't regret it," she said.

Jackson had no doubt that she meant every word. But his gut told him that this investigation was going to test him. He hoped he didn't fail the test.

The waitress slowly approached once again and, at Jackson's nod, she came over to take their orders, even though they'd been so busy they hadn't really looked at the menu.

"The soup and salad combo here is really good. My favorite is the grilled cheese and tomato soup. But if you're hungrier, the French Dip is good, as well," Jackson said.

Rhea nodded. "I'll have the grilled cheese and

tomato soup combo. A little comfort food is always good."

"I agree. I'll have the same, but the full version, Sheila. Some pop also," Jackson said.

"Diet pop for me, thank you," Rhea added, which earned a long look from the detective and a raised eyebrow. The look sent butterflies into flight in her stomach and ignited warmth at her core.

"I've been missing my regular workouts," she offered in explanation.

"What kind of workouts?"

"Is this some kind of interrogation?" she parried, eyes narrowed as she considered him.

He shrugged those broad shoulders. "I just like to know more about the people I'm working with, Partner."

Partner. Rhea liked the sound of that but, other than Selene and a few, very few, close friends, she wasn't used to sharing details of her personal life. But as her gaze locked with his, it occurred to her that the detective wouldn't be satisfied if she didn't answer his questions.

"I normally do a yoga class or two each week, plus some strength training. I also like to take really long walks or hikes when I can."

"In between painting and running the gallery?"

The waitress brought over the sodas at that moment, but once she'd gone again, Rhea answered, "I paint in the early morning and late afternoon when my studio has the best light. I have a full-time manager for the gallery, although I'm the one who decides what to show there."

"I've seen some of your paintings on the website. They're beautiful. Did you always like to paint?"

Rhea nodded and with a laugh said, "My mother said I used to paint myself and Selene with our baby food."

"Is your mom—"

Rhea shook her head. "She and my dad passed a few years ago in an automobile accident. I'm glad, because the worry over what happened to Selene would have killed them."

But Rhea didn't want to revisit Selene's disappearance right now and luckily the waitress arrived with their meals at that moment.

Hunger for the food replaced his hunger for information for the next few minutes, but then he began again.

"I understand. My parents always worried when I was deployed," Jackson said in between bites of the grilled cheese.

"Where did you serve?" she asked and murmured in appreciation of the sandwich, "Delicious."

Jackson smiled and it transformed his face from that of the stern-and-stoic police officer into an almost boyish dimpled grin that made him look much younger.

"I'm glad you like it," he said, but didn't answer her question.

She pressed. "So where was it? Iraq? Afghanistan?"

"Afghanistan. Marine just like my dad."

"Are your parents still alive?" she asked, wondering about her "partner" and his life.

He spooned up some soup, ate it and nodded. "They live in Florida now, close to some of my cousins. Got tired of the Colorado cold, but they come back in the summer to visit."

"Must be nice," she said, thinking of her parents and how much Selene and she had loved to spend time with them.

He nodded and polished off the last of his meal. "It is. I miss them."

"You're lucky to have family," Rhea said wistfully, and Jackson quickly picked up on it.

He raised his glass of soda and peered at her over the rim. "Is it just you and Selene?"

"It is. My parents were both only children, and my grandparents are all gone. It's why it's so important to find her," she said, and Jackson winced as she said it. He didn't believe Selene was alive and didn't want her to get her hopes up, but she'd keep hope alive as long as she could. Because of that, she said, "So, Partner. When do we start this investigation?"

AFTER THEY'D FINISHED LUNCH, Jackson had suggested that they go to his office at the police station, where he'd taken all the materials Rhea had gathered and locked them in his desk for safe-keeping. Especially after what had happened at the inn the night before.

If Matt had been the perpetrator, he might have not only intended to do harm to Rhea, but to also destroy the materials so that the police would not use that information against him.

In the police station, Jackson got Rhea settled in one of their conference rooms so they could discuss her evidence. Normally he would set up a board with all the pertinent information, but since Rhea and he would have to move from Avalon and back, he had created a notebook in the cloud to hold the info, questions and any answers they gathered.

He grabbed his laptop and her evidence and joined her in the room, where he displayed the digital information on a large monitor. As he laid out the hard copies, he said, "I locked these up to keep them safe, but I also plan on scanning everything and adding it to my notes."

"Thank you. I appreciate all your hard work," she said. She splayed her long, elegant fingers, with their teasing rings of gold and silver, against the tabletop, almost as if to still any nervous motion.

As he would with any board he made for an investigation, he talked through the info in the digital notebook, filling in Rhea as he worked.

"There are three possible scenarios. The first is

that Matt Davis murdered your sister. The second is that Selene killed herself. The third is that an unknown suspect murdered your sister."

"And another scenario is that Selene is still alive, and we need to find her," Rhea added. Even though Jackson had only known her for a couple of days, he knew not to argue with her. At least not yet. In time the evidence would eventually rule out that possibility, but he wasn't going to press the issue at that moment.

Pick your battles, he reminded himself.

He went through Rhea's evidence, entering the information into his notes. As he did so, she jumped in with her thoughts to add to the materials. When they finished, it added up to a lot of questions and doubts about the story Selene's husband had provided to officials, making him Number One on Jackson's list of suspects. Which he should have been from the very beginning since the spouse was generally the prime suspect.

But there were also questions about the other scenarios and overlaps. "If there was an SUV by Selene's car that night, and if it wasn't Matt, it's possible that the owner of that vehicle may have something to do with Selene's…disappearance," he said, biting back the murder reference in respect of Rhea's beliefs.

"It *is* possible that SUV is tied to Selene's…disappearance," Rhea agreed, likewise holding back. "What do we do now?"

Jackson rifled through the papers and pulled out her notes on the insurance policies that had been issued barely weeks before Selene's disappearance. Holding up the papers, he said, "How was it that you found out about the policies?"

"I got a call from an investigator from the insurance company. They were doing their own review about Selene's disappearance since the policies were so new," she said and gestured to the bottom of the page. "That's his name and number."

Jackson thought about it for a moment. "Normally most policies are paid out very quickly. At the most, maybe sixty days after the death, but since they had questions, maybe we'll get lucky." He pulled over the conference room phone and dialed the investigator.

"Winston Summers," he answered after a couple of rings.

"Good afternoon, Mr. Summers. This is Detective Jackson Whitaker with the Regina Police Department. You're on speaker and I have Rhea Reilly with me, as well."

"Good afternoon, Detective. Ms. Reilly. How can I help you today?"

Jackson shared a look with Rhea and plowed on. "I understand you were investigating the insurance policies issued to Matt and Selene Davis."

"I was, but we're getting ready to close our

case and pay out the policy on Mrs. Davis," the investigator said.

Jackson detected something in the other man's tone. "You don't sound too happy about that, Winston."

A rough laugh came across the line. "I'm not. I can't prove a thing, but this just doesn't smell right to me."

With a quick sidewise glance at Rhea, whose face had paled with those words, Jackson said, "It doesn't feel right to us, either. That's why we've reopened the case here in Regina."

"Well, you've made my day, Detective. No offense meant, Ms. Reilly. Now that you've done that, I'll tell my superiors to hold off on the payout," Winston said.

Jackson laid his hand over Rhea's and squeezed reassuringly. "I'd appreciate that. If you don't mind, I'd like to tell Matt Davis myself about that decision."

Summers chuckled. "I understand, Detective. I'm sure he won't be happy. I hope that helps your case."

Jackson provided Summers with his contact info and hung up.

Rhea was confused by the investigator's statements. She shook her head and said, "Why will it help the case?"

"It'll make Matt angry and angry people act rashly. They make mistakes, and those mistakes may help us find out what really happened to Selene."

Rhea blew out a breath. "Matt will be pissed, especially if his business is still having problems."

Jackson flipped through her papers again. "You say Matt was having financial issues at the time Selene disappeared?"

She nodded. "Selene had told me business had fallen off and his bills were mounting. That was creating a lot of tension in their marriage." She hesitated, remembering how upset her sister had been, as well as something troubling. "I think that's when I first spotted the bruises on Selene."

"The pressure blew off his lid. Revealed his true nature. Hopefully our visit, and the news about the insurance policy, will do the same. Are you up to going to Avalon?"

Am I up to it? she thought, but then an image of Matt's smug face flashed through her brain. He hadn't even tried to deny the abuse when she'd confronted him shortly after her sister's disappearance.

"I am *so* up for it. If Selene is dead, I'm sure Matt did it, and I want to prove that," she said, her throat tightening as she said the words.

Jackson's touch came against her hand again, comforting and secure. His palm rough, but soothing. "We'll go in the morning."

Which meant she had to spend another night

at the inn. Another sleepless night, watching the doors and windows for signs of an intruder.

"You'll stay with me tonight," he said, almost as if he'd read her mind.

She peered at him, weighing the risk he presented to her in a very different way, but if they were going to see Matt tomorrow, she had to be sharp.

"Thank you, Detective. That's very kind of you."

He raised a hand to stop her, like a cop directing traffic. "Just part of the job," he said, but she doubted that it was standard procedure to take partners home.

When he rose, he grimaced, grabbed his back and stretched, as if to work out a knot. She realized then that they'd been sitting for hours reviewing the case. A second later, his stomach emitted a loud rumble that he tried to hide by covering his lean midsection with his big hand.

"Sorry," he said with a chagrined smile.

"No, *I'm* sorry. I didn't realize how late it was. How about I treat you to dinner?"

He did another stretch of that long lean body and grimaced again. "Actually, I have a nice big steak I was going to cook tonight. How about we pick up your things and we throw the steak on the grill? It's enough for two."

Since she felt like she was already imposing on him, she deferred to his request. "That sounds nice. Thank you."

"Don't thank me just yet. My cooking skills leave a lot to be desired."

She doubted that. Detective Whitaker struck her as someone who was likely quite capable in many ways, which brought a rush of unwanted heat as her mind drifted where it shouldn't. To hide her reaction, she turned her attention to organizing the papers scattered around the table while Jackson scooped up his laptop.

She handed him her notes, and he stood before her uncertainly, his gaze traveling over her face, examining her. But surprisingly, he seemed to misunderstand what she was feeling. "It'll be okay, Rhea. Everything is going to work out."

She went with it, not wanting to clue him in to how uneasy he made her on a personal level. "I know it will," she said and tilted her head in the direction of the door. "I guess it's time for us to go."

Chapter Six

It *was* time to go, and Jackson hoped he wasn't making a big mistake by taking Rhea home with him. But he'd barely gotten any sleep the night before thanks to the intruder at the inn. He needed a clear head tomorrow when they spoke to Matt Davis, which meant he needed to get some rest.

But as he caught sight of Rhea's slim but enticing figure as she walked out the door, his gut tightened with desire, and he wondered just how much sleep he was actually going to get.

In no time they had checked Rhea out of the inn and were at Jackson's home on the outskirts of town. The log cabin home was on a large wooded lot that provided gorgeous views of the lake below and the dam's spillway in the distance.

"This is lovely," she said as she set down her suitcase, walked through his home and out to the large deck that faced the lake.

He shrugged. "Thanks. My dad and I built the place when I got back from Afghanistan."

"You did an amazing job," she said, leaning

against the railing and glancing back toward his home.

"Let me show you to the guest room," he said, walked back in and snared her suitcase. He took her upstairs to a room a few doors down from his and set her things by a queen-size bed. With a flip of his hand, he said, "The bathroom is across the way if you need it. I'm going to get started on dinner."

"Let me help," she said, and they returned to the ground floor where the open-concept space held the kitchen, dining room and living room with a wall of glass that opened to the deck and offered views of the lake, mountains and Regina.

They prepped a salad and sliced up some potatoes and onions to cook on the grill beside a large steak. Since it was still nice outside, they decided to eat out on the deck.

Rhea stood by Jackson as he laid the potatoes, onions and steak on the grill. Contrary to what he'd said earlier, he was quite a capable cook and the meal they ate was simple, but delicious.

Unlike lunch, dinner was a quieter affair, maybe because they had already done a lot of talking during the day. Although Jackson offered an after-dinner coffee, Rhea was eager for some time alone to think about all that had happened the last few days and what would happen in the days to come.

She helped Jackson clean up, but when she offered to help him wash, he demurred. "It's okay. I can handle this."

He could. He seemed to be able to handle a lot, from cooking to building a house. She told herself to have faith that he would handle the investigation of her sister's disappearance as capably.

"Thank you for everything," she said as she inched up on her tiptoes and brushed a kiss across his cheek before making her escape. She noticed his home was almost spartan, but had fabulous bones and stunning views. There were a few bedrooms upstairs, hinting at the fact that the detective hadn't planned on living there alone.

Which made her wonder if he'd built the home with someone special in mind.

She forced that thought away and went to her room. Although it was early, she was tired and wanted to be at her best when they confronted Matt. Closing her door, she changed quickly and got into bed, hoping to make it an early night.

JACKSON STOOD AT the sink, listening for the familiar creak of the floorboards just inches away from the landing and in front of the first bedroom. More than once he'd thought about fixing it, but it served as a very reliable alarm system.

The creak came as Rhea went across the hall to the bathroom and then back, telling him it was safe to head up once he finished the dishes. He took his time, thinking about the materials they'd reviewed earlier, as well as planning an approach to Matt Davis tomorrow.

If Davis was as Rhea had said, he'd be less than pleased about their reopening the case and holding up the insurance payout. He'd push the other man in the hopes of either eliminating Matt from that prime suspect spot or collecting enough evidence to be able to charge him for Selene's murder.

Selene's murder.

Rhea wouldn't handle it well if that's what the evidence proved, but it would at least bring closure. Even if that closure brought pain.

He finished the dishes and went upstairs, careful to step around the creaky floorboards to not wake Rhea. Once he was in bed, he returned to his earlier thoughts, planning tomorrow's mission. The approach and what would follow if Matt's alibis failed to satisfy the many questions he had.

He was just starting to drift off, the plan running through his brain, when he heard the warning squeak that someone was in the hall. A second later, a soft footfall, someone barefoot, alerted him that Rhea was coming down the hall.

His door was open, and he rose up on one elbow as the shadow of her petite figure came into view. She leaned her hand on the doorjamb and, in barely a whisper, she said, "I can't sleep."

JACKSON SAT UP, revealing a broad bare chest with a smattering of chest hair angling down...

Rhea wouldn't think about where that happy trail led, and was reconsidering her visit when he said, "Bed is plenty big, and I've got lots of pillows." He grabbed a couple and laid them down the center of the king-size bed, creating an effective bundling board.

"Thank you. I promise not to be a bother." She hurried to the side of the bed where he wasn't, slipping beneath the sheets. They were smooth, but slightly warm from where he'd been lying earlier.

The bed dipped a little as he settled down again. "Good night, Rhea," he said, his voice husky.

"Good night... Jax."

RHEA WOKE TO an empty bed and the smell of coffee and bacon.

Hurrying, she washed, dressed and met Jackson in the kitchen, where he was forking perfectly crisp bacon slices onto a plate.

"How do you like your eggs?" he said.

She didn't have the heart to tell him she normally didn't eat breakfast. "Whatever is easiest."

In no time, he was cracking eggs one-handedly and scrambling them like a pro.

She poured cups of coffee and asked, "Milk and sugar?"

"Cream and two sugars, please," he said, and she smiled.

"Just like me," she said, earning her a heated look and a laugh.

"Light for sure. A good wind could blow you away, but sweet?" he teased.

She laughed and shook her head. "I can be difficult at times," she admitted.

He lifted an eyebrow in challenge, but she ignored him easily, especially when he laid a plate of eggs, bacon and toast before her and the smells awakened her hunger. She dug into the meal with gusto.

In truth, she was much lighter than she had been six months ago because she hadn't been sleeping or eating well, worrying about what had happened to Selene. Hoping against hope that the feeling inside her that Selene was still alive wasn't wrong.

She was so famished, she finished her plate well before Jackson had finished his, prompting his laughter. "Girl, you sure can put it away."

"And you can sure cook. Thank you."

"You're welcome, but we should get going. Avalon isn't all that far away, but we've got a lot to do."

In a rush, they cleaned up and were on their way to Selene's hometown, which was only about forty-five minutes away from Regina and two hours from Rhea's home and gallery in Denver.

Rhea had done the drive many times before tensions between her and Matt had cropped up and the trips had become one-sided, with Selene only visiting Denver for their girls' weekends.

As they drove, Rhea went over the discrepancies in Matt's alibi. "He said he was gone for only about an hour to check out his client's building location, but I spoke to the neighbors and they said that he was gone for a lot longer. At least three hours if not more."

Jackson shot her a quick glance as he drove. "That gives him more than enough time to do the round trip to Regina."

"And still supposedly 'check out his client's location,'" she said, emphasizing his explanation with air quotes.

Jackson shook his head. "Who goes to a building site at night? I didn't believe it then, but the Avalon officers confirmed the alibi."

"They did, but how much of that was influenced by the officer who works with Matt?" she asked, questioning it the way she had from the very beginning.

Jackson clenched his jaw, clearly not liking her assertion. "I'd rather not think that an officer let a murderer go free on account of a personal relationship."

Rhea scoffed. "You think that's never happened? That it's possible it didn't happen this time?"

Jackson sucked in a deep breath and held it, recalling his chief's words about embarrassing either of the two police departments. But if losing the police chief's job was the price to be paid for the truth, he was willing to pay that price. "Let's not go there until we've run out of options. First thing I'd like to do is talk to Matt and hear what he has to say. After, we'll take a run to the building site. See how long it takes us to get there and then back to Avalon."

"And we can check out the road there also. Matt said he detailed his Jeep the morning after Selene disappeared because it was muddy and he was meeting a client."

Jackson mentally reviewed the evidence Rhea had gathered. "You said the road was paved with gravel."

"It is," she insisted.

"Maybe it wasn't paved six months ago," he offered in explanation, and she shrugged her slim shoulders.

"I'm no expert, but it didn't look like a new road to me. You saw the photos, right," she reminded.

"I did. If things don't add up… I have a friend in the area who has trained dogs," he said, omitting that they were cadaver dogs in deference to Rhea's emotions. But, as he peered at her out of the corner of his eye, it was obvious she'd guessed exactly what kinds of dogs. She worried that full lower lip and glanced away, her gaze shimmering with tears.

"And what then? What if we get nothing from it?"

"We keep on looking, Rhea. I made you a promise and I intend to keep it. We'll go over every fact and every discrepancy. We'll talk to the Avalon police. I called to let them know we were reopening the case," he said.

She shot him a quick look, eyes wide with surprise. "How did that go?"

"They weren't happy. Felt like I was interfering in their jurisdiction, but I reminded them that the Regina Police Department had been involved in the investigation, as well." He reached over and laid his hand on hers as it rested on her thigh. "We have an appointment to talk to them this afternoon."

A deep furrow raked into her brow as she considered what he'd said. Long moments passed until she said, "I appreciate all that you're doing."

He brushed his hand across her cheek and said, "No need for thanks. It's my job." A more difficult one thanks to what he was starting to feel for Rhea.

Returning his attention to the road, he continued the drive to Avalon and the discussion about the case. "Matt started a bonfire that night. It was one thing that struck me as really odd back then.

Who starts a fire and then leaves it unattended for any length of time?"

"And he kept it going almost all night, according to the neighbors," Rhea added.

Jackson nodded, wondering what that might mean. "Matt may have been trying to dispose of..." He hesitated again, sensitive to Rhea's feelings, but that was only making things harder and not easier, so he plowed on. "I'm not sure you can fully cremate a body in a bonfire, but it's something we'll have to check out."

A tired sigh, as if Rhea was carrying the weight of the world on her shoulders, escaped her. "And what if it doesn't prove Matt killed my sister?"

"If it doesn't, we have other scenarios to consider and resolve," he said without hesitation.

"The turn's just in a few miles," Rhea said and gestured toward the highway exit. "Is Matt expecting us? Did you call him?"

Jackson smiled and shook his head. "Matt is in for a surprise. We've got to rattle him, remember?"

Rhea blew out a breath and wagged her head. "Get him angry. Get him to make mistakes."

He jabbed his finger in her direction to confirm it. "You got it. If he's guilty, we will unravel that supposed alibi and get enough evidence to build our case."

MATT DAVIS'S JEEP WRANGLER sat in the driveway, hinting that he was likely at home.

Jackson parked his police cruiser directly in front of the Davis home in a clear line of sight to a big bay window. He cut the engine and shifted in his seat to peer at Rhea. "Are you ready?"

Face a sickly pale, lips pressed tight, she nodded.

"Let's roll," he said as he sprang from the car and around to open the door for her.

Her hand was ice cold as she slipped it into his and they walked to the front door.

He scrutinized the home as they did so, taking in the recently mowed spring green grass. The landscaping was well-kept, and the home spoke of someone who took care of it.

He had barely raised his hand to knock when the front door flew open and Matt Davis stood there, his face mottled with angry red blotches that grew larger as his gaze settled on Rhea. "What are you doing here?" he said, his voice trembling from the force of his rage.

"Matt Davis?" Jackson said and angled himself so that Rhea was partially behind him.

Matt jerked his head up in challenge. "Yes, and who are you? You're not with the Avalon Police Department."

Jackson reached into his jacket pocket, removed his business card and handed it over to Matt, who snatched it away with a swipe of his hand.

Matt shot it only a quick look and said, "What do you want?"

"Detective Whitaker, Regina PD. We've re-opened the Selene Davis case," he said calmly, sensing that the more controlled he remained, the more upset Davis would become.

Matt glared at Rhea. "Why won't you leave this alone? I told you I had nothing to do with Selene's disappearance."

"Just like you had nothing to do with those bruises she had?" Rhea challenged, her voice steady even though Jackson felt her trembling beside him.

Matt angrily jabbed a finger in her direction. "I never touched her. If Selene told you that, she lied."

"She never told me, Matt. I saw for myself. I saw the way you treated her. That's why you didn't want me around," Rhea challenged.

Matt made a move toward her, fists clenched, but Jackson swept up his arm, blocking his access to Rhea. Calmly, Jackson said, "Seems to me you've got an anger problem, Davis."

Matt whipped his head around to nail Jackson with his gaze. "You'd be angry, too, if you were being accused of something you didn't do."

There was a sincerity in the man's response that was unexpected. But sociopaths could be quite convincing, Jackson reminded himself. "If you didn't do it, I assume you'll be willing to answer a few questions."

Davis deflated before his eyes, his shoulders lowering as he took a step back. But then he looked toward Rhea again and jabbed his finger in her direction. "If it means I never have to see her face again, I'll answer any questions you want."

"Where were you two nights ago?" Jackson said.

"Home. Asleep," he said with a nonchalant shrug.

"The Avalon police came by and said no one answered," Jackson pressed.

He shrugged, but met Jackson's gaze head-on. "I sleep with earplugs, and I'm a heavy sleeper. I probably didn't hear them."

The Avalon Police hadn't seen Matt's SUV, unlike today, where it sat in the driveway. He gestured to the Jeep. "Do you normally park in the driveway?"

Matt shook his head. "I normally pull it into the garage, but I'm custom-building something in the garage. I started the project yesterday afternoon."

"Mind showing it to me?"

With a harrumph, Matt pushed past him and to the garage, where he entered a code and opened the door to reveal a number of sawhorses covered with plywood and pieces of a woodworking project.

"Thanks," Jackson said, but pressed on. "Let's talk about the trip to your client's location. You say you went the night Selene disappeared? At night, Matt?"

The other man shrugged and looked away this time, a telltale sign that someone was lying. "I had been at a site all day and, when I came home, Selene and I had a fight. I needed to blow off some steam and went outside to do some yard work."

"You had lots of scratches and cuts on your hands. You told the officers you got them doing the yard work," Jackson said.

Matt nodded. "There were lots of brambles, but I was so mad, I didn't pay attention and got cut up while I piled them in the firepit."

"And then you started the bonfire?" Rhea asked.

Matt glared at her again, but nodded. "I did. I like to keep things looking neat, and it was the easiest way to get rid of them."

Jackson peered all around the house once more and said, "I see that you care, which makes me wonder why you left a live fire to drive up a mountain."

Matt dragged his fingers through unruly waves of blond hair. "Stupid, I know, but I was still too wired after doing that and decided it was as good a time as any to check out my prospective client's building site."

"Up a mountain? In the dark?" Rhea pressed. She had never believed Matt's alibi from the very beginning and nothing had happened that would change her opinion.

Matt glared at her, and spittle flew from his lips as he said, "Maybe if Selene had earned more at that stupid school I wouldn't have had to bust my ass just to keep a roof over our heads."

Rhea was barely controlling her anger. Her body shook with the force of it, but Jackson laid a hand on her shoulder. Gave a reassuring squeeze.

"I understand you were having some financial difficulties," Jackson said.

Matt's gaze narrowed to almost slits and settled on her. More bright splotches of red erupted on his cheeks and down his neck as he said, "I was working out of it. That's why I drove up the mountain. It was a big job and really helped me get things back on track."

Me *and not* us. *It had always been about Matt,* Rhea thought, but kept quiet to let Jackson continue the interrogation. But he surprised her with his next statement.

"That's good to hear, Matt. Especially since I told the insurance company we had reopened the case. They're holding up the payout on Selene's policy until we close the case."

Matt's barely leashed anger turned toward

Jackson. "You had no right to do that. No right," he shouted and leaned toward Jackson, his pose threatening. But he was no physical match for Jackson, who had several inches on him in height and width.

Jackson met him dead-on, his nose barely an inch from Matt's. "I had every right, Davis. A woman is missing. Likely dead and, from what I can see, you had a hand in it."

As he had before, Matt backed down. Bullies couldn't handle being challenged, and it made Rhea realize why Matt hadn't wanted her around. Unlike Selene who hated confrontation, Rhea wouldn't have put up with the way that Matt treated Selene.

"I didn't kill Selene. I don't know what happened to her after she left here that night," Matt said, a defeated tone in his voice.

"If that's true, you'll have no issues with helping us prove that," Jackson said.

Matt gazed away again and nodded. "Whatever you need. I just want to get on with my life."

"Great. We'll be back," Jackson said and exerted gentle pressure on her shoulder to guide her toward his cruiser.

"He just wants to get that insurance money," Rhea said under her breath, not believing a word of Matt's explanation.

"For sure, but he won't get it if he doesn't cooperate to clear his name," Jackson said.

Rhea stopped dead and glanced at Jackson. "You think that's possible? That he didn't do it? That she killed herself?"

"Or that she's still alive, like you hope." His gaze was a dark gray, like a troubled sky, when it settled on her. With a harsh breath, he said, "Anything's possible right now. But, fact by fact, we'll determine what really happened."

Although he had voiced her hope as a possibility, Rhea was certain he didn't believe it likely. But she'd take it for now.

"What's the plan?" Rhea asked, impatient to continue their investigation.

"A trip up a mountain."

Chapter Seven

Rhea had visited Matt's client's site barely a week after Selene's disappearance. She directed Jackson down the highway for several minutes until the turnoff for a narrow gravel-paved road.

Jackson pulled the cruiser off the smooth highway and onto the rougher gravel. The car dipped deeply before beginning the rise to the building site on the ridge.

"This road had gravel when you came up," Jackson said as he drove, navigating past a rut here and there on their journey up the mountain.

Jackson had given her a link to the digital notebook they had created the day before. She pulled her tablet out of her bag and, in no time, she had opened the notebook and navigated to the pages that held the photos she had taken shortly after Selene's disappearance. She held the tablet up so Jackson could see it.

He stopped the car to take a better look at the photos. "Definitely gravel, but not as deep as right now. Do you remember how deep it was?"

Rhea shook her head. "I wasn't thinking about that at the time," she admitted, wishing she had been more observant.

Jackson ran the back of his hand across her cheek. "Don't blame yourself. What you've put together is amazing."

She appreciated his words and braved a smile. She scrolled to other photos of what the site looked like before any construction had taken place. "There was a lot of land cleared along the ridge. Plenty of places and time for him to…"

She couldn't say it and left it at that.

Jackson clearly got it. "Let's go see what's up there now."

They bumped their way up the road to the wide hilltop ridge where Matt was building his client's custom home. A truck was parked before the home's double garage doors. One of the garage doors was open, and a large stack of siding sat there, waiting to be installed.

"Looks like they're almost done with the build," Jackson said.

The home was a large contemporary structure, situated to provide views of the valley below, the town of Avalon and the mountains in the distance.

As they got out of the car, one of the laborers walked over, a puzzled look on his face. "Can I help you?"

"Detective Whitaker with the Regina PD.

We're just here to take a look at the site. Is that a problem?"

Obviously uneasy, the man held his hands up in a stop gesture. "Above my pay grade, Detective. I'll have to check with the contractor." Without waiting, he walked away, whipping out his cell phone as he did so. A short, clearly upsetting conversation ensued, but the man returned and said, "Matt says look away, but don't bother the workers."

Jackson dipped his head and touched the brim of his hat. "Thank you. We appreciate your cooperation."

The man said nothing, only pivoted and returned to work, shouting out instructions to his people who were busy installing the siding.

Rhea brought up the photos again to show Jackson how the ridge had looked before the construction had begun in earnest, since there had already been some digging going on.

Jackson looked around, comparing the site to the photos. With a shake of his head, he said, "The home takes up most of the flat land at this point."

He walked toward the home and backyard, Rhea following. With a sweep of one hand, he held up the tablet with the other and said, "This was all woods. They cleared a good bit to make this open space for the house, the deck and the grass area beyond that."

Rhea nodded. "It was. I remember wondering how big a house they could build without taking down some of the aspens." The thought stormed through her brain again about the aspens being one and feeling the loss.

Jackson tightened his lips and tipped his hat back. "It didn't take that long to get here. When Matt made this round trip, he had plenty of time at this location, but... I can't imagine him burying Selene anywhere on this ridge. Most of the land here would be touched during construction. It's too risky."

A numbing chill erupted inside Rhea at the thought of her sister buried here or somewhere else, and she wrapped her arms around herself. Rubbed her hands up and down her arms to chase away the chill.

Jackson immediately noticed and hugged her. "I want to check out the ridge," he said, and they walked, joined together, to the edge of the property where the land dropped off sharply to thick woods at least a hundred feet below.

"It's more likely he would have dropped her over this edge. The woods down there are dense and probably not well traveled."

Jackson paused and whipped off his hat. He dragged a hand through his hair in frustration. "I don't remember anyone searching that area."

Rhea nodded. "As far as I know, they didn't.

They searched all along the ridge up here, but not below."

"Well, that's where we start tomorrow," he said with a quick nod and urged her in the direction of his cruiser. He paused by the edge of the build site.

Bending, he ran his hands across the gravel. "It's pretty thick. Enough to keep an SUV from getting too dirty," he said as he rose and brushed the dirt off his hand.

She was satisfied by that assessment, but not about any possible delay. "Why tomorrow?" she asked, eager to do the search as soon as possible.

Jackson pulled her door open and she sat, but he didn't join her right away. He leaned his arms across the top of the door and peered away from her as he said, "Today we see Matt again—"

"Why?" she asked, wondering at the reason for another visit.

Jackson met her gaze. "We press on why he spent so much time up here and why he says his car was dirty. Maybe even push him to let us examine his SUV again."

"They found Selene's blood in the house. On the sofa in the living room. Matt claimed it was from a nosebleed," Rhea said and tried not to picture Matt hitting Selene. Hurting her.

"I know it's hard but try not to think about that. We have to stay objective," Jackson urged.

Rhea expelled a sigh. "Objective. She's my sister. A part of me I still feel in here." She laid a hand over her heart.

"I get it. When my sister finally told me about what was happening to her, I wanted to rip the guy apart, but that wouldn't have helped her," Jackson said. "We can help Selene by keeping calm and following all our leads."

He was right, but it didn't make it any easier. However, she would do as Jackson said. Well, for now. She wasn't about to roll over if she didn't agree with what he planned.

"So Matt first. Then Avalon PD. And tomorrow?"

"I arrange for my friend with the dogs to help us scope out the base of the ridge."

He shut the door, walked around and slipped into the driver's seat. Executing a K-turn, he started the drive back down the road. They had only gone about halfway when a shot rang out and pinged against the metal of the cruiser.

"Get down!" Jackson shouted and pushed her down with his hand.

Rhea's heart thumped loudly as she struggled with her seat belt. Another shot and ping rang out. She finally got her belt free and sank even lower, burrowing against the dash and hoping it would provide cover.

Jackson had thrown his door open and knelt behind it for protection as he scoured the area for signs of the shooter. Another shot rang out, coming straight at them. Jackson grabbed his cell-phone and called 911.

"Shots fired! Shots Fired! Aspen Ridge Road."

"Say again," the dispatcher responded.

"Shots fired. Aspen Ridge Road."

Another bullet pinged against the door by Rhea.

"Identify yourself," the dispatcher asked.

"Detective Whitaker. Regina PD. I'm on Aspen Ridge Road. We're pinned down. Shots fired."

"Sending backup," the dispatcher said.

Jackson reached for his own weapon and shouted out to their assailant. "Police! Backup's on the way!"

The response was the roar of a car engine starting up and the squeal of tires as they took off.

Jackson peered at her. "You okay?"

She nodded, unable to say a word, throat tight with fear. Heart pounding so loudly it was almost all she could hear.

Jackson rose, and she screamed out, "Jax, no! He could still be there."

"He's gone, Rhea. It's okay." He held his hand out to help her up.

Jackson swallowed up her delicate hand with his, and it was impossible to miss the violent trembling of her body. She was shaking so hard her teeth were chattering and he yanked off his jacket, leaned in and covered her with it. "It's okay, Rhea," he said again and tucked the jacket around her.

"Thank you," she said, teeth knocking together.

The screeching sound of a siren approached, followed by the crunch of gravel as a cruiser shot up the road until they were in sight of his car.

He held his hands up in the air and walked into plain sight. "Detective Whitaker. I think the shooter took off down the highway."

One of the Avalon police officers exited the car and called out, "Did you see what they were driving?"

Jackson shook his head. He'd been too busy making sure Rhea was safe and taking cover himself to see the vehicle. "Sorry. I didn't."

The officer said something to his partner, who also got out of the car. The duo approached and Jackson greeted them. "Detective Whitaker. Regina PD."

"Officers Watson and Hughes," Officer Watson said, and the other officer added, "You're a long way from home, Detective."

Cops could be territorial, and he got it. No one liked someone else stepping on their toes. "I am. I'm meeting with your chief later about the Davis case. I've got her sister with me," he said and gestured to his cruiser.

The two officers shared a look, and then Watson took a small notebook from his jacket pocket. "How many shots fired?"

"Four. They all hit the cruiser. I was just going to check it out," he said with a toss of his hand toward the vehicle.

They walked to Rhea's side of the car where two shots had hit the passenger door. The road angled at that point, exposing Rhea's section of the vehicle.

"He had a clear shot at your passenger," Officer Hughes said as he knelt by the bullet dings in the door. "Low caliber, as well," he added.

Jackson examined the damage and couldn't disagree. He glanced at the impressions on the door and imagined where the bullets may have ricocheted. He walked to his side of the car and noticed a mark along the dirt wall on his side of the road. He went there as the two officers examined the opposite area and a stand of trees.

He smiled at the glint of metal in the dirt wall. "I've got a bullet here," he called out to the officers.

"We have some damage to the bark but finding anything will be tough. Lots of duff in this area," Officer Hughes said while Watson came over. He took a small evidence bag from his pocket, and Jackson gestured to the bullet.

Watson dug out the slug with a pen knife. Deposited it into the evidence bag. He held it up for Jackson to see. "Definitely a .22. Small caliber, but it could have gone through the doors."

Jackson nodded. "He would have hit Rhea if

that had happened. I wonder why he didn't go through the window or the windshield."

"You think she was the target?" Watson asked, one eyebrow raised in emphasis.

Jackson had no doubt about it. Between the intruder at the inn and now this, someone clearly wanted to scare Rhea off the investigation. Or worse.

He nodded. "She is, but they're going to be sorely surprised. Rhea isn't going to give up until we figure out what happened to her sister."

"We cleared Davis," the officer said, but there was something in the other man's tone that hinted at more.

"Seems like you're not buying the official story," Jackson said.

The officer looked toward his partner, who gave him a "Go ahead" jerk of his head.

"We both always thought the story stunk, but we just couldn't get enough evidence. If you've got it, we're all for you putting that bastard behind bars," Watson said.

Jackson tipped his hat in thanks. "Appreciate it. Right now I think we're going to see that bastard, ask where's he's been the last hour and if he owns a rifle."

"We'll meet you there for backup," Watson said.

Chapter Eight

It had been well over an hour since they'd gone up to the site and returned. Davis wasn't at home when they first arrived but got there within a few minutes.

He appeared confused at the sight of the two police cruisers, but then immediately grew defensive as Officer Watson called out, "Hands on the wheel, Davis."

"I haven't done—"

"Hands on the wheel!" Officer Watson repeated and laid his hand on his holstered weapon.

Matt's gaze skipped across all their faces quickly and then he complied. He looked straight ahead as he said, "What is this about?"

"Do you have a firearm in the car?" Officer Hughes asked.

"No. I'm coming from one of my job sites," Matt explained, his jaw tight and mottled spots of color on his cheeks. His hands clenched and unclenched on the wheel.

"But you own a rifle," Rhea jumped in, and

Matt whipped his head around to nail her with a cold stare. Filled with hate, it sent a shiver down her spine.

"Owned. I had to sell it to pay off some bills."

"I'm sure you did all the appropriate paperwork," Jackson said, and at that, the color on Matt's cheeks deepened and a nervous tic erupted along his jaw. He turned away from Jackson and faced forward again.

"Davis? You got the paperwork?" Officer Watson pressed.

Jaw muscles jumping nervously, Matt said, "No. It was a client, and I didn't want to hassle them."

"I guess you won't mind us checking with him," Jackson said.

Matt's head whipped around again and said, "Her. I'd rather you not bother her. I can't afford to lose a good client."

"Where were you the last hour?" Officer Watson said.

"Like I said before. At one of my job sites. You can ask any of the guys there," Matt advised.

"Trust us, we will. How about you give us the info so we can confirm your story," Officer Watson said, while Hughes jerked his head toward their cruiser to indicate he wanted to talk to them alone.

Rhea walked beside Jax to the car, where the

three huddled together as Hughes asked, "Is there anything else you need right now?"

Jackson glanced at Rhea, who said, "If we can, a look in his trunk would be great."

"You want to look for the rifle?" Hughes asked, but Jackson quickly said, "Blood. I know your office checked earlier, but I'd like to see the trunk for myself."

Hughes shot a look toward his partner and gestured to the back of the Jeep. "Ask him if he minds opening up the trunk."

Watson leaned in toward Matt, who shook his head, but a second later the glass went up and the hatch unlocked with a *kerthunk*. Watson stepped away to let Davis exit the SUV and open the back so they could inspect it.

"I'm going to lodge a complaint. This is harassment," Matt said as Rhea, Jackson and Officer Watson approached.

"This is an ongoing investigation, Davis, and you are the prime suspect," Jackson explained.

Rhea was so thankful for the presence of the officers. She could never have accomplished any of what had happened so far without them.

Matt shot her another withering look, but she refused to let him cow her. She met his stare head-on and raised her chin a defiant inch. Seeing that they weren't going to back down even with his threat, he swept his hand across his open trunk.

"Look away," he said.

Matt and Rhea walked over, and Rhea immediately noticed the difference. "You used to have a liner in here."

A belligerent shrug was his answer until Jackson said, "Where's the liner?"

"Tossed it about a month ago. It got damaged at a job site," Matt said.

Jackson shook his head. "Convenient. Mind if we take a look anyway?"

"Look away," Matt said facetiously.

Rhea watched as Jackson did, using a blue light to check for blood, she assumed. He did it thoroughly, examining every inch of the trunk area and then the ceiling, as well. But nothing showed up.

As Jackson stepped away from the trunk, Matt smiled smugly and crossed his arms. "Satisfied, Detective?"

Jackson tipped his hat back in a relaxed way, but Rhea couldn't fail to notice the tightness along his jaw and the way he clenched his other fist, as if he was barely restraining himself.

"I wouldn't be so smug, Davis. I'm like a dog with a bone and, right now, you're that bone. I'm going to chew you up and spit you out in pieces to get to the truth about Selene's disappearance," Jackson said, voice calm. Maybe too calm.

Matt clearly understood. "I didn't do anything to Selene. She ran away to her," he said and flipped his hand toward Rhea, but didn't stop there. Spittle flew off his lips as he said, "You were always in the way. Always putting foolish ideas in her head. Making her think she was something special. That she was too good for me."

The heat of anger burst into flame in her gut. She stepped toward Matt and eyeballed him, barely inches away. She sensed Jackson and the two officers behind her, ready to move if Matt did, but if anything, she suspected it was Matt they'd have to protect if she lost her control.

In a deceptively neutral tone, she said, "Selene is something special. Something way too good for the likes of you. You never appreciated just how unique and wonderful she is, and I'm glad she finally realized that. And if you think Jax is determined—"

"Jax, is it? Did you charm him into doing this or did you do something else?" Matt said with a snigger.

Jackson stepped toward him, fists clenched, but Rhea laid a hand on his chest to stop him. "We will get to the truth, Matt. And when we do, you'd better hope that you have been telling the truth all along, otherwise…"

She couldn't finish, because she couldn't imagine what she might do to him. She'd never pictured herself as a violent person, but…she wanted to hurt him the way he'd hurt Selene. She wanted him to pay for everything he'd done to her sister.

Afraid she would lose control, she whirled, grabbed Jackson's hand and dragged him back toward his cruiser. At the passenger door, Jackson opened it and then leaned on it, a hint of a smile on his face.

"You got…spunk, Rhea. I kind of like it," he said, surprising her and, before she could respond, he walked to his side of the cruiser, got in and started the car.

"Are we going to see the Avalon Police Chief?" Rhea asked.

"We are. I'm sure by the time we get there he'll know someone shot at us and have heard from Matt," Jackson said. With a strangled laugh he added, "I'm not sure he'll be happy to see us."

For once, Rhea couldn't argue with him.

"THAT WENT WELL," Jackson said and blew out a sharp breath.

"Not," Rhea added with a roll of her eyes.

Jackson leaned against the bumper of his cruiser, tucked his arms across his chest and peered at the Avalon Police Station. With a shake of his head, he said, "At least he promised to check out Matt's story about the rifle."

"Convenient, right?" Rhea asked and likewise took a spot against the vehicle, her gaze also on the stationhouse.

"Especially since it was a .22. The same caliber as whoever was shooting at…us," Jackson said, careful of his words since he didn't want to worry Rhea that someone was targeting her.

Rhea shifted her gaze to him. Her blue eyes were dark, clearly reflecting her concern. "You mean me, don't you? Someone was shooting at me."

With a slight dip of his head, he acknowledged it. "I can't deny that it seems like someone wants you to drop this."

Rhea's gaze skipped over his face, questioning. Almost challenging before she said, "Do you think I should drop this?"

His answer was immediate. "No. The fact that someone wants to shut you up confirms that they're trying to hide something."

She looked away and sucked in a deep breath. In a voice tight with emotion she said, "I'm not afraid of pushing for the truth, Jax."

He ran his hand up and down her back, trying to soothe her upset. "I'm not, either. And to get to you, they're going to have to come through me. I won't let that happen."

She surprised him then by turning into his side, her head tucked against his chest, the gesture so trusting his heart constricted. He splayed his hands against her back and he almost spanned the width of it with one hand, reminding him of how petite she was. How vulnerable.

"I won't let that happen," he repeated and brushed a kiss across her temple.

That action propelled her into moving away from him. She tucked her hands under her arms and shook her head. "This is confusing, Jax."

He had no doubt she wasn't referring to Selene's case. He held his hands up in surrender. "It is, and I'm sorry. It's time we got back to Regina. I've got some calls to make and some more research to do before we return to search beneath the ridge."

"I've got some things I want to go over, as well," Rhea said.

With a nod, he opened the door and waited until she was sitting. "It'll be dinnertime by the time we get back to Regina. How about we get some take-out barbecue?"

"I'd love that. Thanks."

JACKSON'S DINING ROOM table was covered with a mix of spareribs, brisket burnt ends, cornbread, beans, coleslaw, and the photos and papers from Rhea.

Rhea sat at one end with a plate piled with food she had barely picked at, not because it wasn't tasty, but because she was too focused on reviewing materials she had already seen dozens of times in the last six months.

Jackson was at the other side of the table, a nearly clean plate sitting there while he read the papers. As Jackson set the materials down, he took note of her watching him, and of her virtually untouched dinner.

"You need to eat something. We didn't eat all day, and you're going to need the fuel tomorrow for that hike beneath the ridge."

With a quick lift of her shoulders, she said, "I'm not really hungry."

He shot to his feet then, wincing as he straightened. Grabbing his back with one hand, he stretched before coming to her side of the table.

"You okay?" She'd seen him suffer with his back more than once in the last couple of days and wondered if it was from an old injury.

"I am." He gathered the materials at her side of the table and shifted her plate of food directly in front of her. "Eat. Once you do, we can go over this. Again."

Rhea stared at the food and then shot a quick glance up at Jackson. The hard set of his jaw and steel gray of his gaze said he wouldn't budge.

She dug it into the brisket and ate the perfectly cooked meat. It was tender with a delicious barbecue sauce. The taste awakened hunger, as did Jax's promise...or maybe it was better to say his threat that they wouldn't look at anything until she had eaten.

She forked up more meat and, after, beans and coleslaw. Before she knew it, she had cleaned her plate and, as promised, Jackson spread out the materials he had taken away earlier.

Jackson gestured to the police photos of Matt's SUV the afternoon after Selene's disappearance. The Jeep was pristine.

"It rained that afternoon," Jackson said, prompting her for a response.

"It did, but you saw that the road was paved with gravel. There was no reason for Matt to clean it. And why did he get rid of that liner? Because he was afraid someone would find evidence the Avalon Police missed?" she pressed.

Jackson hesitated, obviously uneasy, forcing Rhea to push on. "I'm not afraid of the evidence, Jax. It makes me sick in here," she said and tapped her chest. "It makes me sick to think of Selene dead. Of *how* she died, but we need to be able to talk about it openly."

Jackson pursed his lips and inclined his head, scrutinizing her as if to judge her sincerity. Apparently convinced, he said, "If Matt had Selene in the back of the Jeep, on that trunk liner, it would be hard to get rid of blood evidence."

"Unless she was wrapped in something. A tarp maybe."

He nodded. "Maybe. Or unless he put her in that bonfire instead and didn't take her up the mountain."

"But there were no bones there."

Another slow nod. "And we don't know if it's

possible to do that in a bonfire. I'm researching that in addition to the timeline of Selene's trip from Avalon to Regina." Jackson grabbed a map where Rhea had written in the approximate time Selene had left and been seen by the lake and the exact time that Selene had texted her sister that night.

Rhea ran her finger along a route on the map and said, "Selene had to have stopped somewhere. Maybe more than one place. I did the route a few times to time it, but I'd like to do it again and see what's along the highway."

"First, we search the ridge. And then, depending on what we find, we investigate what's possible with the bonfire. Hopefully by then we'll have something from the Avalon PD about Matt's rifle and the cell phone location information I requested from both Matt's and Selene's provider."

Puzzled, Rhea narrowed her gaze. "Don't you need a subpoena for the cell phone data?"

"Not under ECPA," he began, but paused at her continued puzzlement.

"The Electronic Communications Privacy Act. I don't need probable cause, just sufficient facts to support making the request, and I think you gave me what I needed," Jackson explained.

"Thank you," she said, appreciative of his recognition of all that she'd done.

"We should be thanking you. I feel guilty that I didn't do more at the time, only… Once the Avalon PD cleared Davis, the most plausible explanation was that Selene committed suicide," Jackson said, real apology in his tone.

She laid her hand over his as it rested on the map she had marked up. "I get it, but Selene wouldn't do that. She just wouldn't."

Jackson had had his doubts in the weeks after they'd closed the case and was ashamed that he hadn't done more. But he'd been told to leave it alone and, by then, the winter crush of tourists had kept him busy with an assortment of problems and crimes. Mostly minor incidents, but enough of them that he'd been too busy to give any time to a case his department had closed.

"I understand," he said and turned his hand to take hers into his. He squeezed it tenderly and offered her a compassionate smile. "We will get to the bottom of this. I won't stop this time."

He cupped her cheek with his free hand and ran his thumb across the dark smudges beneath her eyes. "We're both tired. It's time we got some shut-eye."

"Let me clean up." She started to round up the plates, but Jackson stopped her by laying a hand on her forearm.

"I'll get this put away. Go get some rest," he said, intending to not only clean up their dinner, but do a quick walk around his property to make sure all was well.

Rhea was too smart not to realize there was

more to his request, but she complied, and he was grateful for that. He was too tired for another argument, although in the last couple of days they'd seemed to agree more than disagree.

He quickly loaded the dishwasher and went to the sofa, where he'd laid his service belt. Grabbing his flashlight and Glock, he exited his home, careful to lock the door as he did so. Aiming the flashlight, he first searched the woods close to the front door and then did his walk-around, vigilant for signs of any intruders.

Nothing.

Relieved, he went back inside. He turned on a small lamp on the first floor and softly tread up the stairs, careful to avoid the squeaky floor at the landing.

Rhea's door was closed. Jackson hesitated there, wondering if she was okay, but then he hurried to his own bedroom. After showering and slipping on a pair of pajamas, he got into bed and grabbed his tablet. He had reached out to some experts on body cremation and luckily he'd gotten a response. Rhea would not be happy with what the expert had to say.

He added the expert's response to his digital notebook and then skimmed through the remaining emails. His friend with the cadaver dogs had answered that he could assist them the next day. Confirming that the time his friend had proposed was acceptable, he finally set the tablet away for the night.

Time to get some rest because the hike along the base of the ridge would not be easy, both physically and emotionally.

No matter what they found tomorrow, it was going to upset Rhea. He was certain of that. He only wished he could be as certain of what had happened to Selene that night.

Nothing they'd found so far had eliminated her husband in her disappearance. If anything, he remained the prime suspect in Jackson's book.

But with no body, a circumstantial case would be hard to prove. Based on what they had so far, no district attorney would bring the case before a grand jury.

If they couldn't find anything more on Davis, they'd have to push on with the other scenarios.

He just hoped Rhea would be satisfied by whatever they discovered.

Chapter Nine

The sounds and smells of breakfast dragged Jackson from bed. He'd already been up, mentally reviewing last night's response from the forensics experts, as well as what they'd need for today's hike. But whatever Rhea was whipping up smelled just too good.

He threw on clothes and hurried down to find Rhea at the stove, already dressed for the day. He hadn't known what to expect given what she'd worn over the last few days. Loose and very feminine blouses and hip-hugging capri pants.

This morning she was wearing faded jeans and a light sweater that hugged those curves he'd noticed more than he should. Well-used hiking boots, and he recalled that she'd mentioned that she and Selene had regularly gone for hikes. A different side to the talented artist, and one that was more in his wheelhouse. One that was more dangerous for sure, because it was too easy to picture the two of them taking long walks through the woods together.

"Good morning," he said and headed straight to the coffee maker to pour himself a cup. She already had a mug on the counter beside her as she worked at the stove.

"Good morning. I hope I didn't wake you by making too much noise," Rhea said and peered at him over her shoulder.

"I was awake, but those amazing smells forced me to move my butt," he said and ambled to her side to see what she was making.

"I just pulled some things from the fridge. Do you like Mexican food?" she said and, once again, glanced at him, a little apprehensive.

"Love it," he said and passed a hand down her back to comfort her. "It smells amazing."

"Thanks. I figured we'd need something substantial for today's hike." She opened the oven and removed a pan holding corn tortillas filled with eggs and chorizo.

"Take a seat and I'll finish these up." She tilted her head in the direction of the table she'd already set.

He did as she asked and, in a few minutes, she served him a plate with the corn tortillas topped with a red sauce. His stomach rumbled in anticipation, and he barely waited until she was seated to dig in. The flavors exploded in his mouth, and he murmured an appreciative sound. "Delicious. Thank you."

Rhea smiled, her blue eyes alight with pleasure at his compliment. "You're welcome. It's my small way of showing how much I appreciate what you're doing."

"It's my job, Rhea. But I wish we'd done more at first. Known more, like about the domestic abuse," he admitted.

She did the tiniest shrug that barely moved her shoulders. "You couldn't have known. Even I didn't really know, and Selene and I were like this," she said and crossed her middle and index fingers in emphasis.

Despite her all-action clothes for hiking, her elegant fingers and wrists still bore her rings and bracelets. Those feminine touches tightened his gut and had him imagining things best left alone. Especially considering why Rhea was in his home.

"That won't happen this time. We will not leave any stone unturned, but even with that, we may not have enough to charge Matt. You realize that, right?"

The blue of her eyes darkened, and she paused with her fork halfway up to her mouth. "I do, Jax. Trust me, I do."

"Good," he said, hating that he'd dimmed her earlier joy and possibly caused her pain, but he didn't want to set her up for even greater pain by not being realistic.

The exchange created a pall over their meal, and they finished it in silence. Since she was already dressed, Rhea offered to clean up, and Jackson hurried to dress. In no time, he was ready and headed out to his shed to grab a machete. They might need it to clear their way through the underbrush at the base of the ridge. But as he neared, he noticed that the shed door was open.

He reached for his weapon and called out, "Police! Come out with your hands up!"

No sound came from the shed. He approached warily, ready for action as he pulled the door open. He immediately noticed that several items had been moved around, but other than that, everything was as it should be.

He wanted to believe that he'd merely forgotten to shut the shed, but he was the kind of person who had a place for everything, and things were clearly not in the place he'd left them.

Someone had been in the shed.

Matt Davis? he wondered. *Had he followed them back from Avalon to see where Rhea was staying? Had he also been the one at the inn?*

He grabbed his machete, but didn't touch the tools that had been moved. With a quick call to the station, he arranged for his colleagues to dust the tools for prints.

When he returned to the house, Rhea was standing on the back deck, arms tucked tight across her chest against the slight nip in the morning air. "Everything okay?"

"Fine," he lied, not wanting to worry her.

She seemed to see through his ruse, but didn't challenge him.

It took only a few minutes for them to grab some water bottles and their jackets for the hike and hit the road.

RHEA SAT IN silence beside Jackson, wondering what he wasn't telling her. She'd seen the look of concern on his face as he'd returned from his shed. Had he seen something unusual, or was he just worried about what would happen on their hike today much like she was?

She'd been up half the night imagining Selene out in the woods beneath the ridge. Trying to hold on to that belief that her sister was still alive, but even that vision brought despair. If Selene was still out there, what was happening to her? Was she being abused? Was she losing hope that she'd be found?

Rhea would never lose hope, but in that way Selene was the weaker of the two of them. Her mother had often used a Shakespeare quote to describe Selene's spirit. *Swear not by the moon, the inconstant moon, that monthly changes in her circle orb, Lest that thy love prove likewise variable.*

Selene's love had never been inconstant, but she'd been easily swayed at times. Rhea was convinced that was why Matt had deluded Selene about his real character. A character that had convinced Selene to abandon her dreams of being a singer for a more stable profession as a music teacher.

When they found Selene, Rhea would do her utmost to make sure Selene was able to follow those dreams and escape her abusive husband. In a way, Rhea was a lot like the goddess after whom she'd been named. She'd always been a mother figure for Selene and others and would do anything to protect her, much like the goddess Rhea had hidden away Zeus to keep him safe.

She'd been so lost in her musings, she didn't realize they were already close to Aspen Ridge Road until Jackson pulled over just past the turn-off for that street. Parked ahead of them on the shoulder was a pickup with a dog box in the bed. As they stopped, the pickup door popped open and a man in hunting gear stepped out. A second later, two dogs also leaped from the vehicle and followed him to Jackson's door.

The two men shook hands, and Jackson's friend leaned down to peer through the window. He was a handsome Latino with a dimpled smile and eyes the color of hot cocoa. "Good morning, Miss Reilly."

Jackson said, "Rhea, this is Diego. We served together in Afghanistan."

"Good morning, Diego. Please call me Rhea," she said.

"Rhea," he said with a deferential dip of his

head. He glanced toward the woods by the turn-off. "Am I in the right place?"

Jackson nodded. "Our suspect claims he went up to a building site at the top of the ridge. Too easy to find a buried body with all the construction, so we think he did the next easiest thing."

"Tossed her over the edge," Diego said and straightened to scrutinize the area. After he did so, he said, "Let's get going. It may take some time to hike to the spot beneath that ridge."

"I agree," Jackson said and looked at her, his gaze sympathetic. "You ready, Rhea?"

Am I ready for what might lie ahead?

"I'm ready."

THEY HIKED BENEATH the rising wall of the ridge for close to an hour, Jackson ahead of her, hacking through vines and thick underbrush. Yards behind her, his friend Diego gave the dogs free rein to check the area for signs of any decomposition. For signs of Selene. They didn't hit on anything, which was both a disappointment and a relief.

Sweat dripped down the middle of her back and her temples from the heat and humidity in the forest. Sweat lines were visible down Jackson's back and armpits as he cut their way through the forest. In another half an hour, they finally reached a spot directly beneath the building location.

Jackson stopped, sucked in a deep breath and wiped away sweat with a muscled forearm. He shot a quick look at her. "You okay?"

Her legs were trembling, she was a little out of breath and a lot hot, but she shook her head and said, "I'm okay."

Jackson peered over her shoulder at Diego. "How about you, *amigo*?"

Diego smiled. "A walk in the park," he teased. With a hand signal, he set the dogs into action. They scurried into the nearby woods, sniffing here and there, jumping over fallen logs and beneath tangled vines. As time passed, it was clear they weren't hitting on anything.

With a low whistle, Diego summoned the dogs back. "*Nada* here. Maybe we should press on a little more."

Jackson sighed and looked at her. "You okay with that?"

"I'm ready to do anything we need to do." She was determined not to waste this opportunity.

They pushed on, and then in an even wider circle in the area closest to the custom home's location up on the ridge.

But despite all their hard work in clearing the underbrush and hiking through the rough terrain, the dogs failed to locate anything.

It was impossible for Jackson not to see the mixed emotions spiraling through Rhea. Despair. Relief. Disappointment. Hope.

He laid an arm around her shoulders and drew her near. Brushing a kiss on her temple and ignoring Diego's surprised look, he said, "Don't let this get you down. We'll find her."

She turned into him and murmured, "It's just... I don't know. I'm upset, but also relieved, you know."

He knew, boy, did he know. "Let's go grab a bite and regroup. Decide what else we have to do in Avalon before heading home."

Home. His cabin had always felt like home, but with Rhea there now it felt more...complete, worrying him.

It was too much, too soon and, as Diego shot him another questioning look, he realized his friend was likewise wondering what was up.

Rhea nodded, and he released her so they could trudge back through the path they had blazed earlier. By the time they reached their cars, his entire body was bathed in sweat, and his arm was beginning to ache from swinging the machete to cut through the underbrush.

At his cruiser, Rhea stopped and offered a smile to Diego. "Thank you so much for doing this. We really appreciate your help."

"Anything for an old friend," Diego said and clapped Jackson on the back. *Maybe a little too hard*, Jackson thought and grimaced as pain swept across his lower back.

"We do appreciate it, *amigo*," Jackson said,

but sensed his friend wanted a private moment. Especially when Diego jerked his head in the direction of his pickup.

He got Rhea settled in the cruiser. "I'll be back in a second."

She nodded, and he joined his friend as Diego rewarded his dogs and then loaded them into their boxes.

With a quick glance in Rhea's direction, Diego said in a low whisper, "Do you know what you're doing?"

Jackson didn't dare look toward Rhea, afraid he'd reveal too much. He also wasn't sure what to tell his friend. "I know we're trying to investigate her sister's disappearance."

"But that's not all, Jax. It's obvious you have feelings for her," Diego said and finished securing the latches on the dog boxes. He leaned on the tailgate. "Is that going to compromise your investigation?"

"No. I won't let whatever is happening between us change what I have to do."

Diego arched a brow. "Which is?"

"Find out what really happened to Selene Davis."

Chapter Ten

After grabbing a quick bite at an outdoor café, they decided it was worth a go at the building location. They also wanted to look around Matt's home, but Matt refused to allow any inspection without a warrant.

Matt's client was not as reluctant. In fact, he welcomed it.

"I want this all behind me, and would feel better knowing there's nothing going on at my home," he said on the phone.

With that approval, Jackson, Rhea and Diego went to the ridge and allowed the cadaver dogs to roam the property. They were just about finished when Matt pulled up in his SUV and jerked to an angry stop in front of the home.

He jumped from the SUV and came at them, jabbing his finger in their direction. "You have no right. No right," he shouted.

Jackson tucked Rhea behind him protectively and braced for Matt's attack, but at his glare, Matt stopped dead in his tracks. But apparently Rhea wasn't about to hide behind him.

With the spunk he'd come to love, she shifted from behind him and said, "We have every right. We have the owner's permission, because he has nothing to hide."

"I have nothing to hide," Matt said and jabbed his chest angrily.

"Seems to me that if you had nothing to hide you'd let us search your yard," Jackson said and gestured to the dogs who had returned to Diego's side.

"You're six months too late. I'm done with this. I'm done with being harassed. You can bet I'm going to file a formal complaint."

Without waiting for a response, Matt whirled and stomped back to his SUV. Gravel spewed from beneath the tires as he whipped around and raced away.

"Someone's got anger issues," Diego said as he watched the SUV bounce down the road.

"It hurts to think of Selene suffering from that anger," Rhea said, the sheen of tears brightening her gaze. "What do we do if he files a complaint?"

While Jackson liked that it was a "we," he didn't want Rhea to worry. "Let him file a complaint. It won't go far. We'll put together all our evidence for the Avalon PD and see if they can't get a warrant to search the property with the dogs. Especially the bonfire area."

Rhea peered at the animals. "They can identify remains if there's been a fire?"

Diego nodded. "Their sense of smell is strong enough to detect human remains in ashes. Especially if they have a scent to pick up on. Do you have anything with Selene's smell on it?"

With a quick nod, she said, "I do, but back in Denver. Do you want me to get it?"

It was nearly a two-hour trip to Denver, but totally worth the time if Diego's dogs could rely on the scent. "Are you sure about the ashes?" he asked his friend.

Diego nodded. "It's possible, Jax. I can come back once you get the warrant."

With a nod, he looked at Rhea. "I guess we're going to Denver."

It WAS DARK by the time they started the trip back to Regina from Denver. Rhea had picked a number of items that Selene had left behind in her apartment, and then they stopped for dinner since it was getting late.

It has been an emotional day, Rhea thought as she sat in silence beside Jackson. She'd been filled with dread as they'd hiked through the woods. Not finding Selene's body had been a mixed blessing.

When they were almost on the outskirts of Regina, Rhea said, "Thank you for arranging for Diego to help us today."

Jackson shot her a quick look, then immediately glanced in the rearview mirror. "He's a stand-up guy. I knew he'd come if I asked him."

"He served with you?" she asked and, as Jackson again checked the rearview mirror, Rhea likewise looked over her shoulder and saw something way behind them. The lights on the vehicle were off, making it difficult to see it on the dark roadway.

"What is that?" she asked, eyes narrowed as she examined Jackson's face to gauge just how worried he was.

"Nothing good," he said and swept his arm out to press her back against the seat. "Hold on."

He increased his speed, trying to put distance between them and the vehicle that was racing toward them. In front of them, a slow-moving lumber truck blocked the road, and they were on a section of highway that made it difficult to pass.

Jackson muttered a curse beneath his breath and slowed. He shot another look in the rearview mirror, and she did the same. The unknown vehicle was advancing on them. Too quickly.

Inching into the lane for opposing traffic, Jackson whipped back behind the truck at the sight of lights coming toward them.

He splayed his hand across her upper chest and said, "Brace yourself."

The first hit against the back of the car sent her reeling forward and back, while Jackson battled to maintain control, working the steering wheel to stay on the road. Hitting the brakes to stay away from the back of the lumber truck and the logs that would break through the windshield and kill them.

A second jolt had the cruiser swerving, fighting against the momentum sending them toward the truck and a fatal collision.

Jackson swung the wheel into opposing traffic, searching for an escape, but the threat of lights coming toward them drove him back behind the truck again.

He shifted to the open shoulder and hit the gas. Gravel pinged against the underside of the cruiser. Another ram almost sent them off the shoulder and into the woods beside the road.

As soon as Jackson cleared the truck, he swung in front of it, earning a loud blare of the truck's horn as he cut if off. He used the truck as a shield for their rear, but the vehicle that had been chasing them switched tactics.

While riding on the shoulder, the vehicle smashed into the side of their car, sending them into the opposing traffic. It swung into the lane, blocking their way back onto the right side of the road, leaving Jackson little choice but to race onto the far shoulder. It was much narrower and, as he did so, the cruiser sideswiped a number of trees until he jerked to a rough stop.

Their attacker sped away, any view of them blocked by the slow-moving lumber truck.

"You okay?"

Am I? she wondered, finally taking a deep breath. Her heart pounded so powerfully in her chest it echoed in her ears.

"I'm okay," she said, forcing calm into her voice even though she was anything but.

The lumber truck had stopped, and the driver exited the cab and came racing over. Jackson lowered the windows on the cruiser to speak to him.

"You folks okay?" he asked, leaning in through Rhea's window.

"We're okay. Did you get a plate number on the vehicle that hit us?" Jackson asked.

The trucker shook his head. "No, sorry. I was too busy trying to control the truck. All I can tell you is that it was a Jeep Wrangler. Red, I think."

Jackson and Rhea shared a look. "How about the driver?" Rhea asked.

The trucker tossed his hands up in apology. "No, sorry. Didn't see him."

"Mind if I get your contact info before you go?" Jackson asked and, without hesitation, the trucker pulled out his wallet and handed Jackson his license. Jackson snapped a photo and handed it back to the man, who ambled to his truck and took off.

Jackson grabbed his radio to call in the incident, but they were in a dead zone. Same for their cell phones.

Grumbling, Jackson said, "We'll have to drive closer to town to get a signal. Are you sure you're okay?"

Rhea blew out a rough laugh. "As okay as you can be when someone tries to kill you."

Jackson brushed the back of his hand across her cheek. "Davis is obviously angry that you're not letting this alone."

"I won't let it alone until we know what happened to my sister," Rhea said, no doubt in her voice despite the fear that had filled her barely moments earlier.

Jackson smiled. "That's my girl."

She wanted to say she wasn't his girl or anyone else's, but in truth, it felt good. She felt good. Protected despite all that had happened in the last few days. Jackson would keep her safe, but she was no damsel in distress. She'd keep him safe, as well.

The cruiser, damaged and worse for wear, could be driven, and Jackson pulled back onto the road.

In less than fifteen minutes they had arrived at the Regina Police Station where Jackson had to file various reports regarding the attack. While he did so, Rhea sat beside his desk, sipping on a coffee someone had been nice enough to bring over.

Despite the heat of the liquid, a chill had settled into her center as she considered that someone had tried to kill them.

Matt? she wondered again, despite the call to the Avalon police who had confirmed that Matt's Jeep was sitting in his driveway with a cold engine and nary a scratch on the vehicle.

A gentle hand on her knee pulled her from her thoughts. "I'll only be a little longer," Jackson said.

She nodded. "It's not a problem. Take whatever time you need." She didn't think she could sleep anyway once they got home. Cradling the coffee mug in her hands, she let it warm her cold fingers and still the slight tremble.

Less than five minutes later, Jackson shuffled all the papers he'd been working on into a neat stack, shot to his feet and held his hand out to her.

Without hesitation, she slipped her hand into his and rose unsteadily from the chair. He grabbed hold of the coffee mug from her other hand and set it on his desktop.

A gentle tug on her hand urged her close, and he wrapped an arm around her. Hips bumping as they walked, they left the station and walked to a different cruiser. The first one was now evidence.

Once she was seated, she wrapped her arms around herself, shock still filling her center with cold. "We're going to find out who did this," Jackson said and rubbed a hand across her shoulders.

"I know," she said, confident that Jackson would keep his promise.

Jackson started the cruiser, turning up the heat and, little by little, the cold left her thanks to a combination of the warmth blasting from the vents and Jackson's presence.

Another police cruiser sat in the driveway of his home.

Jackson waved at the young officer behind the wheel and the officer waved back, confirming he had their attention.

"He'll be there all night," Jackson advised, and it offered some comfort.

"Thank you for all that you're doing. I know it wasn't easy for you to buck your chief."

Jackson cupped her cheek. "It wasn't easy, but everything that's happened just confirms there's more to Selene's disappearance."

Rhea wouldn't read more into his use of *disappearance* instead of *murder* or *suicide*. There still wasn't enough to substantiate her belief that Selene was alive. But there was certainly enough to prove that whatever both police departments had believed might be wrong.

"Do you think Matt had anything to do with what happened tonight?" she asked, certain that her sister's husband had to have been the one who'd driven them off the road.

Jackson blew out a breath and swiped his thumb across her cheek. "He's my prime suspect, but if he did it, it was with another SUV. If he does own another one, we'll find it."

With another gentle caress, he said, "Let's get some rest."

She nodded and met Jackson at the front bumper. She tucked herself against him, wanting to not only draw comfort from his presence, but to offer it, as well.

When they entered, she had no doubt where she'd be sleeping that night.

Beside Jackson.

Upstairs they separated only long enough to change, but she went straight to his room and slipped into bed beside him. Turning, she laid a hand on his chest. His skin was hot beneath her palm, and she cuddled close, laying her head against him. But despite that, she felt restless with too many thoughts racing through her brain.

He eased his arm around her and splayed a hand across her back to hold her close. He soothed it up and down and said, "You need to shut it down and get some rest. Tomorrow is going to be a long day."

She raised her head to peer at him. At the strong, straight line of his jaw, stubbled with his evening beard. "I can't stop thinking about all that's happened. All we still have to do."

He shifted until they were almost eye-to-eye. Until his nose bumped hers and his breath warmed her lips. His body was hard beside hers.

Strong. The body of a warrior with the scars to prove it, she realized, noticing the shine of old scars along his shoulder and upper arm.

She raised her hand and ran the tips of her fingers along it, her gaze on those injuries before skipping up to meet his.

"Shrapnel from an IED. Kandahar province."

He said it matter-of-factly, but there was no missing the tension that crept into his body.

"Did you lose anyone?" she said and stroked her hand across the scars, wanting to soothe him the way he had her so often in the last few days.

"We avoided the worst of the blast and didn't lose anyone. Didn't lose anyone on my tours of duty and brought everyone home," he said, pride evident in his tone.

She had no doubt his leadership was part of the reason. That kind of leadership would have been coveted anywhere, which made her wonder why he had chosen Regina.

"Was Regina home for you?" she asked, wanting to know more about the man who was unexpectedly becoming a part of her life. A man who was tempting her at a time when she needed to be focused on only one thing: finding her sister.

He nodded. "I grew up in Regina, and my parents lived here until they moved to Florida. It's a safe place that I want to keep safe so I can raise my kids here."

Kids. She wondered if there had ever been

anyone he'd wanted to have his children and the question escaped her before common sense could silence her.

"No one special," he said. "Before now," he quickly added and locked his steely gray gaze on her. He cradled her cheek and traced the outline of her lips with his thumb.

Her heart skipped a beat, and her breath trapped in her chest. The rough pad of his finger was a powerful caress and jolted her core alive.

"Jax," she eked out past the knot in her throat.

"Relax, Rhea. It's too soon, and we have too much to do," he said and tempered his touch, releasing her gaze and shifting his hand to the back of her skull to draw her close. He massaged her head tenderly, easing past the charged moment. Bringing some peace as her mind traveled from thoughts of the past and Selene to those of a happier future. One possibly spent exploring whatever was going on with Jackson. Maybe kids. Maybe a little shop along the quaint street in Regina. A Matt-free Selene finally doing what she loved.

Rhea's light snore and the softness of her body along his confirmed she had fallen asleep. It brought a smile and relief to Jackson.

It had been a difficult day and night with all that had happened. Tomorrow would be no less stressful.

Even though they had picked up clothing from

Rhea's apartment that hopefully had enough of Selene's scent to examine the bonfire ashes, unless Matt consented they'd have to wait for a search warrant. Regardless of that, he'd done enough research to recreate the bonfire Matt had kept going all night.

Hopefully that recreation would provide the information they could use to either charge Matt or get the search warrant they needed.

And if not…

Jackson refused to consider that possibility. One way or another, he'd find out what had happened to Selene that fateful fall night.

Chapter Eleven

Jackson examined the circle of pavers that his friend Declan had recreated from the crime scene photos. A large pile of wood sat a few feet away, ready for a fire.

"What do you think?" Declan said, arms crossed as he also scoped out his work and shot a quick look at Rhea.

"It looks like Matt's firepit," Rhea said and strolled around the circle, likewise scrutinizing Declan's work. "Thank you so much."

"Anything for my friend Jax," Declan said and clapped Jackson on the back, making him wince from the force of the blow.

"Easy, dude," Jackson warned and eyeballed Rhea, hoping she hadn't caught his pain, but she had.

"Sorry, dude. I forgot," Declan said. He gestured toward the back of his restaurant. "I'm going to go get the hog, okay?"

Jackson forced a smile. "That would be great,

and thanks again for helping us with this. Let me know what I owe you—"

"No way, dude. I owe you big time," Declan said, raising his hands to stop Jackson from insisting on his request.

"Well, thanks," he said and watched as his friend returned to his building to fetch the pig carcass they were going to cremate.

"You okay?" she asked. Laying a hand on his shoulder, she gently skimmed her hand from his upper arm to the middle of his back, as if trying to soothe his pain.

He nodded, his lips tight against both the slight sting that lingered from his friend's exuberance and admitting weakness to Rhea. "I'm okay. I still have pain sometimes from the shrapnel damage."

Turning into him, she surrounded him with her arms and hugged him, providing comfort and peace he hadn't felt in quite some time. Not since before Afghanistan.

The moment was shattered as Declan and one of his workers returned, arms wrapped around a large hog that roughly weighed the same as Selene. They wrestled the carcass to the center of the firepit and dropped it. It landed with a thud, kicking up dirt. Making Rhea jump with the sound.

He returned her embrace, hugging her close. Peering at her, he said, "Are you ready to do this?"

She shook her head. "No, but there's no choice is there? Not if we want to know if Matt did this to Selene."

Before he could warn Rhea not to get her hopes up, she was in action, making a pile of brush and kindling above the hog. As she started to expertly stack the logs, he joined her and said, "I see you've built campfires before."

"Selene and I were Girl Scouts. We started a lot of campfires in our day," she said, adding more wood to the tipi atop the hog.

He helped her, adding logs and tinder until the body of the pig was almost completely covered.

Jackson stepped back, hands on his hips as he scrutinized their prospective campfire. Rhea joined him, staring at the pile and then up at him. "What do you think?"

"I think it's ready." He reached into his pocket for the box of matches and, once the match was lit, tossed it into the tinder material. The first hint of flame quickly flared into more. Smoke came from the pile along with the crackle and snap of wood igniting. The fire had taken.

Satisfied, he headed to the trunk of the police cruiser where he'd stowed two portable camping chairs. Rhea and he set them up several feet away from the campfire. The heat quickly built from the intensity of the flames, but they still had to keep it going for several hours, much like Matt had done the night of Selene's disappearance.

Rhea was silent as they sat there, staring into the flames as they consumed the pig. The smell of the meat roasting was awkward. While there was no denying it was pork, it made her wonder…

No, better not to wonder, she told herself.

Jackson shifted from his chair to add more logs and keep the fire going. It had barely been an hour, but the greedy flames were quickly eating up the wood on the pile, as well as the carcass beneath the ash and embers. Because of that, Jackson walked over to an area with wood waiting to be split, grabbed an ax and went to work.

He swung the heavy ax with ease the same way he had chopped with the machete the day before. He was clearly a man used to physical labor, despite the injuries that still seemed to bother him. Over and over he swung the ax, the thunk of it hitting the log loud in the quiet of late morning.

Feeling guilty, she rose and went over to collect the split wood and add it to the pile by the fire. Tossing more logs into the firepit as well to keep the flames going.

The physical labor helped to keep her mind off what was happening in the firepit, but it also whet her hunger. Especially as Declan's restaurant opened for lunch service and the smokers that they'd loaded up that morning were opened, spewing the tasty smells of barbecued meats into the air.

Almost as if he'd read her mind, Declan exited from the back of the restaurant with a large tray loaded with food and drinks. He brought it over and placed it on a stump by their chairs. "I thought you might be hungry by now."

"Thank you. That was very thoughtful," she replied.

Declan did a side glance at the firepit as Jackson approached. "I know this is a tough thing for you."

She nodded. "It is, but your help has really made it easier."

Declan shrugged. "Like I said before. Anything for Jax…and for you since…well, you and Jax." He stopped, clearly uncertain and possibly uneasy as Jackson returned from splitting logs.

With a laugh, Jackson wagged his head. "Deck, you always manage to talk too much."

"And before I stick my foot in my mouth even deeper, I'm going," he said as he jerked a thumb in the direction of the restaurant and backed away.

Rhea smiled at the friendly and jovial exchange between the two. "I guess you've known each other a long time."

Jackson chuckled, sat and reached for one of the plates that Declan had brought out. "You might say that. We grew up together, but then I went off to college and Deck stayed to help his family with the restaurant."

"Have they had it for long?" The building was

well-kept and had that look of age that hinted at permanence.

"A few generations." Jackson took a big bite of the brisket sandwich Declan had provided.

"Where did you go to college?" she asked, wanting to know more about the man who was intriguing her on so many levels.

"Annapolis," was his one-word answer around a mouthful of pulled pork.

She picked up her own sandwich, grateful it was beef and not pork. She nibbled the burnt ends, murmuring her approval. "Delicious."

With a nod, Jackson took another big bite. After swallowing, he said, "His pops taught him well, and Deck really upped his game. He's won quite a number of competitions over the years."

Rhea admired the pride that Jackson had in his friend, as well as the fact that they had been friends for so long. Much like the permanence of the restaurant, it spoke to Jackson's character and the fact that he was a man you could count on. But then again, he'd more than proved that over the last few days.

"You were a Marine?" she said, resuming her earlier quest for information.

"I *am* a Marine. Once a Marine always a Marine," he said with a smile.

Yet more proof of his ability to commit. "And then you came home and became a cop?"

With a small shrug, he swallowed the last of

his sandwich. "I wanted to serve, and it seemed like the best place to do it."

In a town the size of Regina, she imagined crime was usually limited to minor incidents, which was why Selene's case had been such a big deal at the time. "It must be pretty quiet in Regina for the most part."

He placed his plate back on the tray and did another shift of his shoulders. "It is. Problems with people partying too much. Noise complaints. Shoplifting. Occasionally a burglary or assault."

"Cat up a tree," she teased, imagining him dealing with a dowager and her felonious feline.

Jackson laughed as she'd intended. "More like bear up a tree. Those suckers can really climb," he said, but then he grew a little more serious. "I like it. I like dealing with people. Solving problems. If I become chief…"

There was something in the way his voice trailed off that warned there was an issue there.

"Are you next in line?" she asked, wondering about his hesitation.

"I was…am," he said with a little more confidence, but she sensed his concern. When he shot her a hurried, almost furtive glance, she realized she was the cause of that worry.

"Your chief was going to blow me off, wasn't he?"

"Let's just say he wasn't sure there was enough evidence to reopen the case." Jackson rose and tossed more wood on the bonfire before returning to his chair.

He was in major avoidance-mode, but she wasn't going to give up until she had her answer. "But you decided differently, and he didn't like that."

Heaving a sigh, he nailed her with his gray gaze, now almost charcoal with his upset. "You know you would have made a great interrogator."

She met his gaze. "I suspect you think I'm more like a Grand Inquisitor. But I don't give up, which is why we're sitting here, trying to cremate a hog."

"It is," he admitted with a slight dip of his head.

"But that put you in hot water. Maybe even enough to affect you becoming chief?" She hated that she might be the reason Jackson's career was at risk.

His demeanor was deadly serious as he said, "If it gets to the truth of what happened to Selene, it's worth it, isn't it?"

She nodded. "It is."

"And you remember your promise, right?" he pressed, turning the tables on her.

She remembered, as much as she might not like accepting that Selene was truly gone. "I do, Jax. I remember it every time we hit another brick wall."

Jackson nodded and worried that today's experiment would turn into another disappointment for Rhea. With that in mind, he said, "I reached out to people who might know more about cremating bodies."

She tilted her head and focused on him, her gaze both questioning and challenging. "Does that mean you don't think this is going to prove anything?"

He hesitated, but had to be truthful. Especially since he'd already kept his problems with the chief secret. "It may prove something you don't want."

"Which is?" she urged and gripped the arms of the seat with hands white with pressure.

Gesturing with his hands, he mimicked the path of the flames in the bonfire. "With those low paver walls, we're getting a lot of flames, but the energy of the fire is being expended upward."

A deep furrow marred her brow. "What does that change?"

He once again used his hands to illustrate what he'd learned. "If the fire was contained, like in a barrel or a pit with higher sides, you'd get more heat in a concentrated area."

Her eyes opened wider and she nodded, getting what he was saying. "We may not have enough heat to cremate…"

She couldn't finish, and he didn't push on that point. "Bingo." He reached into his pocket and pulled out his smartphone. He opened up his digital notebook with the crime scene photos of

Matt's bonfire. Leaning close to Rhea, he held the phone so she could see, although he suspected they were tattooed on her brain.

"There's a lot of ash here, but nothing else."

"He could have taken away anything that was left."

He couldn't deny that. "He could possible remove larger bits of bones, but getting rid of other—"

"What other?" she countered.

"Body residues. Teeth," he said, but she held a hand up to stop him, the sheen of tears glistening in her gaze.

"I don't want to upset you—"

She cut him off again with a quick wave of her hand. "I get it, Jax."

He had no doubt she did, but just in case, he reviewed what Matt had done that night. "He started a bonfire and went up to the ridge location."

"Supposedly. He could have also followed Selene to Regina."

Jackson drilled back to the pages in his digital notebook on the timelines Rhea had worked out. Analyzing them, he said, "He could have. It's only about forty-five minutes to Regina, and the neighbors say he was gone for a few hours."

Losing some of her earlier upset, Rhea jumped right into helping him work through the materials. "We have two witnesses who place an SUV near Selene's car."

With a nod, he ran a finger across his screen, scrolling through the notes and then thought out loud. "Let's say he and Selene did fight. She storms off. He's pissed and needs to literally burn off his anger. He starts the bonfire. But he's still really pissed at Selene and needs to do something about that."

Rhea joined in. "He goes after her to give her a piece of his mind. There's really only one way to Denver, and it runs right through Regina. He finds her. They fight again and something happens."

Jackson wagged his head. "But it's possible Selene took longer to get to the lake than everyone originally thought. We'll have to investigate that. But let's assume he ran into Selene right away. Why not just toss her body in the lake?"

"We'd find Selene right away in the lake, wouldn't we?"

Jackson immediately knew where she was going. "Which is why you think she may still be alive. Because otherwise we'd have found her body in the lake." He paused for a moment and then quickly added, "Unless the spillway was open to keep the lake levels in check."

She whipped out her phone, and her elegant fingers danced over the smartphone screen. With a satisfied dip of her head, she held it up for him to see a report she'd obtained.

He'd only done a quick glance at it before, but now he took her phone, used his thumb and forefinger to zoom the image. Rhea had filed a Freedom of Information Act request to obtain information on spillway activity from the department that managed it.

"Spillway was closed that night and for days after. If Matt put Selene in the lake—"

"Or if she killed herself—which she didn't— we would have found her body," Rhea finished.

The crackle and thump of logs collapsing in the fire drew his attention. Embers shot up and danced in the air as more wood fell in the center of the pit. "Time for more logs."

Together they piled on even more wood and, as they did so, it was obvious to Rhea that there was a little less of the pig carcass beneath the ash and embers.

She snuck a peak at her watch. "It's been about four hours since we started."

Jackson likewise did a quick look at his phone to confirm the time. "About. We'll need to keep it going a while longer to match what Matt did."

"Which means more time to get to know each other," Rhea said, wanting to find out all she could about Jackson.

"First, more firewood," he said and walked over to split more wood.

She recognized avoidance when she saw it, but she refused to let him avoid that talk. He was becoming too special to her in just the few days they'd spent together. Too hard to resist, even though becoming involved with a man was low on her priority list. Both before and after college she'd been focused on establishing her career. Once it had taken off, her emphasis had shifted to her gallery. In the years since then, she'd made a number of friends and spent time with Selene, but a relationship…nonexistent.

That she was giving the "relationship" label to what she was feeling for Jackson was a scary proposition. He was connected to too much hurt. He was also nothing like the artsy men who inhabited her life. But maybe that was why she found him so interesting. He was the epitome of the strong, silent hero type, but beneath that hard surface was a powerful and compassionate man.

Instead of sitting, she walked to where he was working and, as he split the logs, she picked them up and carried them close to the firepit. They had just finished making a nice pile when Declan came out of the restaurant with another tray, this time loaded with what looked like slices of pie and tall glasses of lemonade.

"Dude, if you're in the mood to keep on chopping, I could use some hickory for the smokers," Declan called out and motioned to a far pile of wood with the tray.

Jackson nodded. "Sure thing. Least I could do to thank you for all your help and the food."

And to avoid talking to me, Rhea thought, but bit her tongue. He could run, but he couldn't hide.

When Jackson moved to the pile of hickory logs, she tagged along, picking up the pieces he'd split to add them to the neat pile Declan had beside the uncut logs.

"You've known Declan forever," she said, hoping to start the discussion on what was hopefully a safe topic.

Jackson raised the ax and sent it flying down onto the log, splitting it in half. "We grew up in the same neighborhood. Went to school together."

"I bet you were a jock," she said, picturing him on a football field.

Jackson grinned and shook his head. She thought she heard him murmur, "Grand Inquisitor," but then he said, "I was. Baseball, not football."

It was too easy to imagine that powerful and lean body in a tight baseball uniform, igniting heat at her core. But he was more than just a pretty face.

As she picked up a pile of cut hickory logs, she asked, "Why does a landlocked Colorado boy decide to go to Annapolis?"

Jackson set the ax on the ground and stretched, arching his back and wincing slightly. But before she could offer to help, he picked up the ax and went back to work.

She pressed him for an answer. "Why Annapolis?"

He finished quartering the log and set the ax aside, obviously in pain. But he finally answered her. "I didn't want my parents to have to pay for college since they still had my sister and brother to worry about. Dad is a Marine and I wanted to follow in his footsteps. Annapolis made sense."

She stacked the last of the logs he'd split and followed him back to the fire. Together they tossed on more wood, then sat to eat the slices of pie Declan had brought out. But that wasn't going to keep her from her goal.

"Are you always so sensible and responsible?"

Chapter Twelve

He paused with a forkful of apple pie halfway to his mouth and glanced at her. His steely gray gaze glittered with a heat she hadn't thought possible. "Not always."

The warmth that had kindled in her core earlier grew ever higher, like the flames in the fire a few feet away. It was so intense, she had to cool off with a few sips of icy lemonade.

"What about you, Rhea? I know you're talented. Determined," he said, the latter word followed by a playful chuckle.

She considered him over the lip of the glass, thinking about how to answer. After a pause, she said, "I know some people think artists can be temperamental and flighty. You probably did."

He smiled as he scraped the last of his pie from the plate and then licked the fork clean. "I plead the fifth," he joked, but then quickly added, "But you probably thought I was uptight and by-the-book."

She felt the urge to shake him up a little. "I still do, but I look forward to you proving me wrong."

His glass rattled against the tray as he set it down and, when he fixed his gaze on her, it seared her with its fire. "I look forward to that also."

She gulped down the rest of her lemonade to cool the blaze he'd ignited and turned her attention to her pie. Another collapse of the logs in the bonfire had them both bolting from their chairs to the wood pile. They almost collided there, forcing Jackson to reach for her to keep her from falling over.

Electricity sparked between them, and Rhea rushed back to her seat.

Jackson took his time feeding the fire, needing to control what he was feeling for Rhea. Banking the flames burning inside because he worried that if he released them, it might consume him. He was unused to such feelings, being, as Rhea had said, normally uptight and by-the-book.

But Rhea had loosed those bounds he'd lived with all his life, first as an athlete, then as a Marine and finally as a cop.

It couldn't have happened at a worse time, he thought. Rhea's emotions were too fragile, and he had to stay focused because so much was at stake, including his career. But more importantly, he had to keep Rhea safe.

His Crime Scene Unit was working on the

cruiser, trying to get paint and metal samples in the hopes of identifying the vehicle that had attacked them. They were also trying to locate any CCTVs along the route that might also yield more information. The Avalon police were determining if Matt owned any other SUVs that fit the bill and still trying to get a warrant to search his property.

With a cruiser parked in front of his own home, he hoped that would be enough to safeguard Rhea.

The vibration of the cell phone in his pocket warned that they'd hit the time limit for their bonfire.

"Is it time?" Rhea asked.

He nodded. "We need to let it die down and see what we have."

"I'm ready, Jax. No matter what happens, I'm ready," she said and met his gaze, hers unwavering and filled with the kind of determination he'd come to expect from her.

"We'll be ready, Rhea. And if this doesn't work out, we'll move on," he said, wanting to reassure her.

"I know." She reached across the short distance separating their chairs, holding her hand out to him.

He grasped her hand and twined his fingers with hers. The comfort he offered her with that touch rebounding to bring him peace, as well.

It took another hour for the fire to die down enough for them to check out what had happened.

Jackson grabbed a shovel that Declan kept for feeding and controlling his smoker fires. Carefully, he shifted the still red-hot embers in the firepit, moving them away from the center to try to expose what, if anything, was left of the pig carcass. It was hot work, and sweat bathed his body from the heat.

As he moved the embers toward the edges, he had to take a step back to cool off.

Rhea was immediately there with another tall glass of lemonade.

"Thank you," he said. He swiped his forearm across his brow to wipe away the sweat and chugged down the drink.

After a few deep breaths, he resumed shoveling the embers until he had revealed a large portion of the carcass. Or at least what remained.

He stood beside Rhea, hands on his hips, staring at the pile of bones in the center of the pit. A dark residue, probably from the animal's fat, stained the area around bones that were relatively intact. Some spots near the edges, where the fire hadn't been as hot, still had minute remnants of flesh. Ashes and embers circled the pig remains close to the pavers.

Maybe if they allowed more time for it to cool down, the central section with the bones might be closer to the crime scene photos that the Avalon Police Department had taken in the days after Selene's disappearance. *But is it close enough?* Jackson wondered.

"It's not similar, is it?" Rhea said, dejection obvious in every line of her body. Her shoulders drooped, and deep frown lines were etched beside her lips. The blue of her gaze was dark, like the lake waters during a storm.

He eased his arm around her shoulders and tucked her close. "Let me get the embers back in place, add another pile of logs and then let the fire die out naturally. We'll come back later to check it out and, if that doesn't do it, we move on, right?"

She nodded and, in a tiny, hardly audible voice, she said, "We move on. I'll get you another drink."

Rushing away, he watched her go, aware she was barely holding it together. He quickly returned to work, piling the glowing embers back into the center of the pit. He added another mound of logs and hoped that by doing so the end result might support continuing their investigation of Matt because the other alternative...

Rhea didn't want to believe that Selene had killed herself. He found it hard to believe, as well, but no one knew why someone would choose such an end. Why they didn't ask for help and kept it bottled up until the emotions were just too much to handle.

The sound of a footfall drew his attention, but it wasn't Rhea. It was Declan, with another tall glass of icy lemonade and deep furrows across his brow.

"Your...friend is... Maybe it's time you guys went home. Took a break. I can finish up here," he said with a flip of his hand in the direction of the fire.

Jackson hated to leave their experiment unfinished. But as he looked at Declan's face, his friend was obviously as worried about Rhea as he was. "Do you mind us leaving it here until later?"

"Until tomorrow, Jax. You need to take a break. A long one," he said and clapped him on the back, gently this time.

In truth, whether later or tomorrow it wouldn't matter. Not to mention that the ache he'd been feeling off and on in his back all day was blossoming into major pain. "Tomorrow," he said and followed his friend into the restaurant where Rhea was sitting in one of the booths.

The lunchtime crowd had died down, and Declan's staff was getting ready for the dinner rush.

He eased into the booth across from her and their knees bumped beneath the table. He laid a hand on her knee. Squeezed reassuringly. "How about we head home?"

She nodded, but remained silent, her face flat. Shoulders still fallen.

Declan hurried over and laid a pizza box on the

table. At Jackson's questioning look, his friend shrugged and said, "Figured you might not want to cook dinner."

Jackson rose and bro-hugged his friend hard. "Thanks for everything, Deck."

His friend dipped his head in Rhea's direction, urging Jackson into action.

Jackson held his hand out, and she slipped her hand into his, but peeled away for a moment to hug Declan. "Thank you. We really appreciate all that you've done."

"Anything for friends," Declan said as he embraced her.

"Let's go," Jackson said, and Rhea seemed only too eager to leave. He understood. Their experiment was leading them on a path to other scenarios.

One of which included Selene's suicide.

Normally he'd be relieved when he eliminated one scenario during an investigation and moved closer to solving a case.

He felt no such relief today.

The short ride to his home was quiet, but Rhea's disappointment was almost palpable. In just two short days, they'd eliminated the idea that Matt had disposed of Selene's body at his client's location and probably the possibility that he'd cremated her in his firepit.

But that didn't eliminate Matt or their other

scenarios, including the one where Selene was still alive.

"Matt could still be a suspect," he said, but as they pulled past the police cruiser stationed in his driveway, instinct said something was wrong.

"Stay here," he said and opened his door while unclipping the thumb strap on his holster. As he did so, the smell of smoke drew his immediate attention. A slight breeze carried smoke from beyond his home.

He leaned down and drew his backup Glock from his ankle holster. Bending, he held it out to Rhea and said, "Do you know how to use this?"

Rhea took the gun from him and pushed the button to remove the magazine and check it before slipping it back in. "I've got it."

"Good. Stay put."

Rhea eased the safety off the Glock and watched as Jackson walked toward the police cruiser. When he got there, he immediately acted, reaching in for the radio and calling for an ambulance.

The hackles rose on the back of her neck, and she hoped the officer wasn't badly injured.

She searched the area in front of the home, but the fading light of dusk and the tree line around the home created too many shadows. But her gaze caught on a brighter swirl of white above the home. Smoke.

No, not Jax's home, she thought and opened

the door. The smell of smoke was impossible to miss now and, as Jackson rushed around the edge of his home, gun drawn, Rhea couldn't just sit there doing nothing.

Ignoring Jackson's instructions, she dashed from the cruiser, gun in hand. Following the path Jackson had taken, she ran into him as he stood on his deck, pulling a garden hose from a reel. He ran with it toward the shed. Licks of flame were just beginning to escape from a broken window at the front of the structure.

Jackson turned the hose on the shed, trying to keep the fire tamed. He had holstered his gun and was radioing with his free hand. She walked over and took the hose from him, and he mouthed a "Thank you." With his hands free, he drew his weapon again and finished calling for the fire department since the garden hose was barely keeping the flames at bay. If they spread to the deck or to the pines behind…

She didn't want to think about the fire destroying Jackson's home because of her. *Because of me.*

Keeping the hose aimed on the flames, she also kept her eyes and ears open for signs of anything out of the ordinary. Like the scream of sirens approaching and the lights flashing through nearby woods. Reds and blues escaped through the underbrush and tree branches as police cars, an ambulance and a fire truck raced up the road.

The crunch of gravel and pounding footsteps signaled that help was on the way. Jackson joined her a second later and said, "Whoever did this is long gone."

"I'm sorry, Jax. How is the officer?"

"Awake. He thought he heard a noise, opened his window to investigate and got cold-cocked. EMT is with him, and it seems like he'll be okay," Jackson explained and held his hand out for his backup weapon.

She returned it, and he strapped it back into his ankle holster. As he did so, he asked, "How did you know how to use the Glock?"

"Dad was a cop. He taught us how to safely handle a weapon," she explained and began to hose down the edges of his deck as the heat of the shed fire warned it was in danger.

Luckily, a crew of firefighters dragged a fire hose from the front of the house and turned a burst of water on the shed, beating back the flames. But the fire had done major damage to the structure, and it collapsed with a loud crash, sending embers flying all around.

The firefighters moved closer to douse the burning remnants, as well as the area all around, to avoid the spread of the fire.

Rhea stood there, more worried about Jackson losing his home than the likelihood the fire had been set because of her. Jackson came up behind her, wrapped an arm around her upper body and drew her against his chest. She went willingly, the comfort and security of his arms welcome.

The firefighters shut off the water and walked over to inspect the remnants of the shed. One of them shook his head, tipped his hat back and walked to where they stood. He glanced at Jackson and said, "Can't say for certain yet, but I think an accelerant was used."

"I kept gasoline in there for the chain saw and mower," Jackson advised.

The firefighter took a look back toward the shed and nodded. "Probably used that, since it was handy. We'll know more once the arson investigator has his look at it."

"Thanks, Max. You guys did an amazing job," Jackson said and leaned over to shake the man's hand.

"Appreciate it, Jax. Sorry this happened to you," he said and shot a look at Rhea, as if wondering if she was the cause. Rousing her guilt again about what had happened.

Jackson and she followed them to the driveway, where the EMTs were pulling away and Jackson's colleague was standing by his car, chatting to the police chief.

"Stay here and, this time, do it," Jackson said and reinforced his instruction with a slash of his hand.

Since the chief shot her a look that was both

annoyed and concerned, she decided to stay put as Jackson had instructed.

Jackson spoke to his injured colleague and the police chief in hushed tones, making it impossible for her to overhear what was being said. The chief waved to officers standing by another cruiser, who joined them as discussion resumed.

Not long after, the injured officer got into his car and pulled away, and the police chief did the same, leaving the one cruiser with the duo of officers. Jackson spoke to them for another few minutes. With a series of handshakes and some backslapping, the conversation ended, and Jackson returned to her side.

"Are we good?" she asked, wondering at what they'd planned.

"We're good. They'll stay all night and run hourly checks on the grounds," Jackson advised and opened the door on his cruiser to remove the pizza Declan had given them.

At her questioning gaze, he said, "Dinner. A man's got to eat."

Despite his comment, he handed her the pizza box at the front door and said, "First, a quick check through the house, although I doubt whoever did it is in here."

"Why?" she wondered aloud.

"If they really wanted to do damage they'd have torched the house. The shed was intended to be a warning," he said and, once again, drew his weapon.

He didn't need to say the words. His warning glance rooted her to a spot by the door, pizza box in hand.

She waited, patiently, as Jackson did a sweep of his living room, dining room and kitchen, and then went up the stairs. Long anxious moments later he came bounding down the stairs, his gun holstered once more.

"All clear," he said and took the pizza from her. But as they entered the house, the smell of smoke on them was powerful.

She wrinkled her nose and said, "I think I'd like to shower and change."

Jackson sniffed the air, as well, and said, "Me, too. I'll get this in the oven while we shower."

"Thanks," she said and rushed up the stairs and through her shower.

She beat Jackson to the kitchen, scrounged through his refrigerator to make a salad and set place mats and cutlery on the breakfast bar, trying to stay busy. Keeping busy was definitely a way to keep from thinking about the fact that someone was trying to stop their investigation.

Was Matt that desperate? she wondered, but didn't have time to dwell on it too much as Jackson came into the kitchen in a T-shirt and sweats. The T-shirt hugged hard muscle, and the sweats hung loose on his lean hips. Her brain went somewhere dangerous, especially as he came by to snag a piece of lettuce from the salad and brushed against her.

He smelled of soap and man. All man, but she had to contain that awareness of him. It was just too dangerous, too distracting, considering all that was happening. But try as she might, it was impossible to ignore his presence. Powerful. Comforting. Tempting in a way that no man had ever tempted before.

And surprisingly, despite all that had happened that day, hunger awoke as Jackson pulled the pizza from the oven. He cut the slices with a big knife, his movements competent. Almost elegant, which made her itch to sketch him. She'd been so crazed in the last couple of days she hadn't even touched her sketch pad, but maybe she'd try tonight.

If Jackson would model for her, that was.

Working together as if they were an old married couple used to routines, she served the salad and he brought over the pizza and sodas. A glass of wine might have been nice, but they had to stay alert, not to mention that a little wine might make him even more dangerous to her control.

The pizza was delicious and unusual. "I've never had grilled pizza with barbecued chicken before."

"It's one of Deck's specialties. People love that

he turns things on their heads," Jackson said and stuffed the last bit of crust into his mouth.

"He's been great. Please thank him for me," she said, grateful for all that Declan had done.

Jackson leaned back in his chair and focused his gaze on her, his eyes locked on her face. "Your dad was a police officer?"

She nodded and nibbled at the pizza crust. "He was. My mother was a music teacher, like Selene."

Jackson dished out the last two slices onto their plates and said, "I guess that explains the information you gave me. It was as neat and complete as any case file I've ever read."

"Dad was a stickler for being orderly and for doing the right thing," she said with a lift of her shoulders.

"That also explains why you're so determined to make things right for Selene," he said, grabbed his slice and took a big bite.

Although she picked up her own slice, she held it before her, unsure how to answer without having him worry. But he'd been nothing but honest with her, even admitting that assisting her might cost him the position as chief. So she charged on. "The only thing that would make things right is to have Selene home again, Jax. That's what I want more than anything."

Jackson set down his slice and this time when

he gazed at her, the gray of his eyes was almost charcoal with worry. "I know you want that—"

She raised her hand in pleading. "Let's just leave it at that. Please."

He did as she asked, finishing the rest of his slice in silence while she nibbled at hers.

They washed dishes much the same way, standing side by side in silence, Jackson washing and Rhea drying. When they were done, Jackson leaned against the counter. "It's not that late. What would you like to do?"

It came out of her mouth before she could stop it. "I'd like to sketch you."

Chapter Thirteen

Jackson lifted a brow. "Sketch me?"

She mimicked drawing on paper with her
hands. "It helps me relax."

It might help her relax, but being the object of
her attention would do little for his peace of mind.
Still, it had been a challenging day for her, far
more than for him, so if it would help her, he'd
suffer it.

"If it'll help." He pointed toward his living
room. "Mind if I start a fire?" he said, even
though between the bonfire and the shed destruction he'd almost had enough of flames and wood
smoke. But, as night had fallen, a chill had settled
in the air and in him.

One of her dark brows flew upward, as if questioning his sanity, but seeing that he was serious,
she acquiesced with a tilt of her head. "I'll get my
sketch pad and pencils."

She rushed out and, if Jackson was reading her
right, she was anything but relaxed. Despite that,

he intended to go along with her request, no matter how dangerous it might be to his self-control.

He marched to the living room, determined to get this over with as quickly as possible. Since he always kept the fireplace ready, it took little time for the tinder to catch and spread flames to the logs neatly stacked above it. Much like Rhea's dad, he was also a stickler for being orderly and doing the right thing. Which meant, no matter how tempting Rhea might be, he had to control himself.

At the wall of windows facing the deck, he hit a switch to engage the privacy blinds built into the panels. He didn't normally use them, preferring to see the woods and stars beyond, but the last thing he wanted was for a colleague doing his rounds to see him modeling for Rhea. He'd never live it down with his friends at the station.

She returned to the living room with her sketch pad and pencils, and took a spot in a chair directly opposite his big leather couch. "Would you mind stretching out there?" she asked, peering at the couch.

He stretched out there often after a hard day at work, the fireplace lit and the television turned on to one of the fix-it channels or a baseball game. But doing so for her...

Sucking in a breath, he lay down and spread out on the couch, his toes touching one arm while he tucked a pillow against the other arm and set his head down on it.

Half-facing her, he tried to inject comfort into his voice as he said, "Here I am. Draw away."

A half smile, the smile of a siren luring men, graced her lips while she flipped open the pad and grabbed a pencil. "Would you mind…?" She didn't finish, only did a little wiggle of her finger that communicated her wishes.

Despite being filled with trepidation, he pulled off his T-shirt. She rose and shut off the light on the table beside him, leaving only the firelight for illumination. It created intimacy in the room. Maybe too intimate since desire seemed to catch and flare like the tinder and logs in his fireplace.

Instead of returning to her chair, she sat on the edge of the coffee table and skimmed her hand over his shoulder to adjust the position of his body. But her touch changed as she ran her hand along the muscles on his arm and down his side, getting lighter. Even hesitant, but it did nothing to quell the passion rising within him.

He grabbed her hand to stop her, but found himself twining his fingers with hers and drawing her close. "I thought you wanted to sketch me?"

With a big swallow, she said, "I did. I do."

"The wisest thing would be for you to sit back in that chair and draw," he said, his voice husky to his ears from the strain of not pulling her close.

A light huff escaped her before that siren's smile drifted across her lips again. "That would be the right thing to do. So would this."

She leaned down and covered his mouth with hers, her lips mobile against him. Wet. Warm, so warm.

He cradled the back of her head to keep her near as they kissed over and over until they were both breathless. And while he wanted to urge her down beside him on the couch, he mustered his last bit of self-control.

Sweeping his hand around to cradle her jaw, he applied gentle pressure to shift her away. He locked his gaze on hers, a turbulent navy blue with desire. "I want this… I want you."

She nodded, clearly understanding where he was going. "You do the right thing. *We* do the right thing."

Clapping her hands on her thighs, she shot to her feet and sat across from him. She snatched her sketch pad from where she'd laid it earlier, picked up her pencils, crossed her legs and leaned the pad on her knee.

Rhea worked furiously at first, pencil scratching against the paper as the initial lines of the drawing took shape. The rough shape of the sofa. The long lines of his strong body, lying there with tension in every muscle. The power nestled in the shadows between his thighs…

"Relax," she said and inhaled deeply to do the

same, slowing the stroke and pressure of her pencil to add dimension to the drawing. She normally did landscapes and still lifes, rarely portraits, but she was pleased by the image slowly coming alive on paper.

"You look...pleased," he said, a sexy huskiness in his tone.

She was and flipped the pad so he could view the drawing.

He raised an eyebrow. "Is that how you see me?"

She turned the pad around and examined her work. The man in her sketch was passion personified, his gaze heavy-lidded. A sexy smile on his lips that promised the pleasure she had experienced barely minutes earlier.

"Yes," she answered without hesitation.

He shifted to sit, fingers laced together, forearms leaning on his muscled thighs. His features were troubled, his brow furrowed and his gaze nearly black. "I think it's time for me to do another walk around the property and check in with my colleagues."

Without waiting for her response, he grabbed his T-shirt and jerked it on. Pushed to his feet and marched off. After the snick of the front door opening and closing, Rhea leaned back in her chair and sighed.

What am I doing? It was crazy to get involved with Jackson, and not just now, when all their focus and attention had to be on the case. She had her life in Denver that she loved. The gallery, her apartment and the vibrant city life. But she couldn't deny that despite Selene's disappearance in Regina, the town called to her with its beautiful downtown, homes and the surrounding countryside. And, of course, Jackson. She wanted to explore what she was feeling for Jackson, both emotionally and physically.

And he clearly felt the same.

He wanted her and she him, but it would have to wait.

She collected her drawing supplies, determined to avoid Jackson. Determined not to crawl into bed with him. This time it wouldn't be because she was afraid or needed comfort. When she did join him the next time...

Driving that image from her brain, she bounded up the stairs and to her room. As she did so, she heard the front door open and close again, as well as the grate of the lock. Glancing toward the stairs, she caught sight of Jackson and closed her door. It was the coward's way out, but she didn't trust herself not to give in to what she wanted.

Jackson.

Leaning against the door, she took a bracing breath and listened for his footsteps as they came near and stopped by her room. A long pregnant pause followed, but then the footsteps moved away, down the hall to Jackson's bedroom.

The breath rushed out of her. Arms wrapped around her sketch pad, she walked to the bed and quickly changed into her pajamas. As she slipped into bed, she took hold of her sketch pad and opened it to the drawing of Jackson. Ran her fingers over it, imagining it was his skin beneath her hand, but not tonight.

Closing the pad, she grabbed her tablet, too wired to go to sleep.

With a few quick strokes, she was in Jackson's digital notebook. As she did, the program notified her that Jackson was likewise reviewing the information, and she shook her head.

In some ways, we're too alike, she thought and gave herself over to considering the evidence. Again.

THE LITTLE ICON at the top of the menu indicated that Rhea was likewise logged on to the notebook with the case file.

It seemed almost silly that they were both working on the materials separately, yards apart, but Jackson understood. Being together right now was too dangerous.

With the evidence they'd gathered in the last few days, it pointed to the possibility that Selene's death may have happened in Regina and not Avalon. He opened the file with the information that detailed the witness accounts of Selene's visit to the lake and the possible presence of a second vehicle.

First, he reviewed the approximate times against the spillway activity logs Rhea had obtained. The spillway had opened for a short stretch of time early that night, but even with adjustments for possible witness error as to the time Selene had been at the lake, the spillway had likely been closed when Selene had been killed.

If she'd been killed, the little voice in his head challenged.

Despite that being one of the possible scenarios, it just didn't seem plausible. If she had run away from Matt, Jackson had no doubt she would have run to her sister.

And then there was the text she'd sent.

I can't take it anymore. I can't. I'm finally going to do something about it.

What had that "something" been? he wondered. Had it been ending her life? If it had, the timing of that text would put her by the lake. Wouldn't she just have walked into the lake to take her life? Especially since her purse and cell phone had been sitting in her car, supporting that supposition. And if so, they were back to the fact that her body should have been found in the days after her disappearance.

He and his colleagues had searched the lake

and surrounding shores with a fine-tooth comb and had not found her nor any evidence of her.

Blowing out a frustrated sigh, he opened his nightstand and pulled out the pad and pen he kept there because he often got ideas about cases at the oddest times.

He switched to the page in the notebook with information on the timeline for Selene's trip from Avalon to Regina. Setting aside the laptop, he took the notes and transferred them to his pad of paper, confirming what they had discussed before, namely, that Selene had spent way more time on the road between leaving Avalon and arriving at the lake in Regina.

Since he was well familiar with the route, he listed a few places Selene might have stopped that night. Since Selene had rushed off according to Matt, she might not have been prepared for a trip to Denver. That possibly meant a stop for gas.

There were two different gas stations near Regina to check in the morning.

She might have also been hungry or thirsty. Maybe tired and needing a pick-me-up, like a cup of coffee. There was a general store and coffee shop right off the highway, as well as two different restaurants on the street leading to the lake.

He jotted down those names and, for good measure, grabbed his laptop and searched the route using one of the online mapping services. That had him adding a chain pharmacy location, as well as a local pub. It was the kind of place a single woman might go for a quick hookup, but Selene would not have known that. She also would not have known that on occasion a rougher crowd frequented the location.

A chirp on his phone alerted him to a message.

She had to have stopped somewhere along the route to the lake. Maybe the coffee shop. She's a caffeine fiend.

He texted back, I agree. I made a list of spots we can check in the morning.

A long pause followed before she texted, Thank you. I appreciate all that you're doing.

He wanted to say that it was his job, but it had become more than that to him. *She* had become more to him.

Fingers over his phone screen, he hesitated, but then finally wrote, We will find out what happened. Together.

Breath held, he waited for her response and smiled when it came.

Together. Good night, Jax.

Good night, Rhea.

Chapter Fourteen

Morning came way too quickly.

Jackson woke just as the first rose-and-purple fingers of dawn were clawing their way into the sky. He dressed in his uniform, strapped on his service belt and chatted with the two officers in the cruiser.

"Nothing happening, Detective," said the one young officer.

"Thanks, Officer Troutman. I'm going to take a walk around the property, just in case."

He reconnoitered the grounds, but everything was in order, except of course for the burned shed, including the charred remains of his favorite chain saw and ax.

When he went back inside, Rhea was also dressed and putting up a pot of coffee.

"Good morning, Jax," she said, glancing over her shoulder at him.

He walked to her and laid a hand at her waist, urging her around. "Everything okay with us?"

She peered up at him, her blue gaze skimming

over his face, as powerful as a caress. "We're…
okay." With a flip of her hand in the direction of the
stove, she said, "I was just going to make breakfast before we checked out some of those stops."

"One of the places, the general store, has a 24-
hour cafeteria. Since you're up, how about we get
breakfast there? The food is really good."

"That sounds great. We could also poke
around. See if anyone remembers seeing Selene,"
she said and went to leave, but he tightened his
hold at her waist to keep her close.

"Don't get your hopes up. Luckily, we'll have
that cell phone information I requested later
today. That should help us pinpoint Selene's and
Matt's whereabouts on that night."

"I get it, Jax. Don't get disappointed that nothing we've done so far has helped us know more
about what happened to my sister. I get it," she
said, the threat of tears obvious in her voice and
eyes, which shimmered with angry tears.

He wasn't going to push anymore. "I'll wait
for you outside." He eased his grip, and she raced
away to get her purse.

He went out to his cruiser to wait for her. When
she approached, he held the door open and waited
until she was settled to get behind the wheel for
the drive to the general store.

Rhea tried to stay patient as Jackson drove,
even though her insides were as turbulent as
water boiling for tea. She hadn't meant to sound

condemning but knew it had come out that way. But it wasn't Jackson's fault that they hadn't made any progress on the case. Well, not unless you counted ruling out scenarios as making progress.

But she was sure of one thing: If Matt had killed Selene, he hadn't taken her back to Avalon. Everything at the ridge construction site and the bonfire seemed to point to that. But everything inside of her continued to say that Selene was still alive. Rhea still felt her presence strongly and maybe in the next few days they would get the evidence needed to prove that.

The general store was on the road immediately adjacent to the highway. If Selene had taken the exit for Regina, she would have driven down that road on her way to the lake.

Much like everything else in Regina, the general store was a quaint throwback to earlier times. Way earlier times, like the 1800s. It had that old Western feel to it with a retail area where you could buy an assortment of items. Right beside the retail section was the restaurant area, complete with waitresses in neat candy-striped aprons that screamed 1950s instead of 1850s. Both areas were neat, clean and busier than she had expected at such an early hour.

As soon as they walked into the restaurant, one of the waitresses, a pretty twentysomething with dark brown hair, doe eyes and a brilliant smile hurried over to greet them. Well, greet Jackson.

"Nice to see you again, Jackson," she said and literally batted her eyelash extensions at him while barely flicking a glance in Rhea's direction.

"Nice to see you, too, Melissa. Table for two please," he said and smiled at Rhea. For good measure, he laid a possessive arm around her waist.

Melissa's smile immediately faded as she stared at Rhea and at Jackson's gesture.

"Right this way," Melissa said and, with jerky motions, pulled menus from a nearby holder.

They followed the young woman to a booth. After handing them the menus, Melissa rushed off with a muttered, "I'll get you some coffees."

Rhea stared after the waitress and raised an eyebrow. "Old flame?"

"Unwanted crush," he answered without hesitation and buried his head in the menu.

As handsome as Jackson was, she suspected he was the object of quite a lot of crushes, including her she had to admit. Although it was well past the crush phase and into the "What do we call this now?" point in a relationship.

To distract herself from where those thoughts would go, she perused the menu, which reminded her of one from a diner she had visited during a trip to New York City. There were dozens of menu choices, from a variety of omelets, pancakes and waffles to assorted breakfast wraps. Maybe too many choices, but Jackson had said the food was good here.

The noisy clatter of china and cutlery heralded Melissa's return as she set their cutlery and coffees down before them. She whipped out a pad and pen. "What can I get you?"

"Cream. Sugar. Huevos Rancheros, please," Rhea said and handed the menu to the waitress.

"Rocky Mountain wrap for me. Thanks, Melissa," Jackson said and likewise returned the menu. Before she could walk away, Jackson said, "Do you ever work the nighttime shift?"

She shook her head. "Going to night school, so I'm always on either the morning or afternoon shift." She jerked her head in the direction of another of the waitresses. "Judy over there sometimes works late night."

"Would you mind asking her to come over?" Jackson said and offered up a smile that seemed to restore some friendliness to the waitress.

"Sure thing, Jax. Anything for you," she said, stevia-sweet, but with a frown in Rhea's direction.

She sped away to place their orders and talk to another waitress, who was just hanging up her apron behind the counter. The older woman glanced in their direction, but seeing that it was Jackson, smiled and waddled over. She was at least six or seven months pregnant.

When she approached, Jackson popped up from his seat and offered it to her, but she waved him off. "If I sit down, I may never get up again," she said with a tired laugh, laid a hand at her waist and stretched.

Jackson chuckled and slipped back into the booth. He reached into his shirt pocket and pulled out a photo of Selene, which jerked a puzzled look to Judy's face. The pregnant waitress looked from the photo to Rhea and back to the photo. Rhea explained.

"She's my twin sister. She disappeared six months ago."

Judy nodded. "I remember. Her photo was all over the papers and on the news."

"Were you working that night?" Jackson asked.

Judy nodded. "I normally work those late shifts. Lets me be home for the kids during the day. She wasn't in any night that I was working."

"You sure?" Jackson pressed and slipped the photo back into his shirt pocket.

Judy tightened her lips and wagged her head. "Very sure. We don't get that many people late at night during the fall months. More in the summer and winter. If I'd seen her, I would have contacted you back then."

"Thanks, Judy," he said.

Rhea parroted his words. "Thank you. We appreciate it, and good luck with the new baby."

"Thank you, and hang in there. You're in good hands," Judy said with an incline of her head in Jackson's direction.

"I know," she said as Judy waddled out of the restaurant.

At that moment, Melissa returned with their orders, and Rhea understood why Jackson's dish had been called the Rocky Mountain wrap. The wrap was huge and piled high with french fries, gravy and cheese. Not that her eggs were much smaller. A big pile of scrambled eggs were topped with fresh salsa and cotija cheese, and the smells...

Her stomach rumbled from the aromas of spice, fresh cilantro and the earthiness of the coffee.

"These are gut busters," she said, but dug into her eggs.

"Perfect," Jackson said with a wink and likewise forked up some of his wrap because it was way too big to eat with his hands.

Hunger tamped down any discussion for several minutes, but Rhea realized she'd never be able to finish. There was way too much food, no matter how tasty it was.

Jackson seemed to have no such problem as he continued chowing down. She hated to interrupt his enjoyment of the meal, but after Judy's comments, she'd been wondering where else Selene might have stopped the night she disappeared.

"My sister loves her coffee. If she was in a hurry, but tired, she might have stopped for a shot of caffeine to keep her going."

Jackson nodded. "It is another hour and a half to Denver, so that makes sense. We'll try the coffee shop next while we wait for the cell phone location information."

Rhea leaned back into the booth cushion and rubbed her belly, which she was sure was at least an inch bigger thanks to the delicious breakfast. "I feel like I need a nap and we just woke up," she said with a laugh.

Jackson grinned and chuckled. "I know what you mean, but I can't say no to the Rocky Mountain wrap," he said and kept on eating while she sat there, watching him and thinking about where else her sister may have stopped.

If Matt had attacked Selene, had she had fought back? If she had done that, had she been hurt? Had she stopped at an urgent care facility or a pharmacy for some supplies? Rhea wondered. All places for them to check, and she knew Jackson had placed the big chain pharmacy on his list. She felt confident that Jackson had things under control. That she was in good hands, as Judy had said.

And such nice hands, she thought, as he laid down his knife and fork when he finished his meal. She was a sucker for hands, and she had to admit that his touch, so comforting and strong, stirred intense emotions within her.

He raised his hand and signaled for Melissa to bring over the check.

"Let me," Rhea said, and Jackson was about

to argue with her, but apparently seeing her determination, he demurred.

"Thanks, Rhea," he said and laid his hand over hers.

Comforting and strong, she thought again and took hold of his hand. "I should be thanking you for offering your time. Your home. Your protection."

JACKSON WANTED TO say again that it was his job, but that would be a massive lie. It had become so much more than that. But he had to maintain his objectivity, which had slipped more than once in the last few days. Because of that, he tried to adopt a neutral and professional tone as he said, "It's what I had to do to help solve this case."

Her hand jerked in his, obviously stung by his words and tone. She awkwardly drew her hand away and hid it beneath the tabletop. When Melissa brought over the check, Rhea barely glanced at it before placing her credit card on the plastic tray. Melissa swept by and snatched it off the table, clearly still in a huff.

Great, two women pissed at me, he thought. His cell phone vibrated and chirped in his pants pocket, and he drew it out to see a message from the desk sergeant.

Just emailed you info from cell phone company.

He texted back, Great. Thanks.

He swiped to open his email and smiled at the data the cell phone company had provided. Not only was there a spreadsheet for the week Selene had disappeared, the company had assigned one of their engineers to interpret the data.

Rhea was tucking her credit card back in her wallet when he said, "We have the info. I suggest we head to the police station to review it."

"That's good news," she said and slipped out of the booth.

He followed Rhea to his cruiser. It took only a few minutes to reach the police station and settle themselves in the conference room. With a few commands, Jackson had the spreadsheet and analysis on a large monitor.

His police chief strolled by the room, then backtracked to enter. The older man gestured to the information. "Is that the cell phone data?"

Jackson nodded. "It is, and we also have a report that pinpoints where Selene and Matt were that week."

With the laser pointer and mouse, Jackson reviewed the data and maps with Rhea and his boss. The information confirmed exactly when Selene had left Avalon, but more importantly, where she had stopped that night. The tracking continued after Selene's message to Rhea, but since the cell phone had been left behind in the car, it told them little about what had happened after the text.

Still, the data showed that there had certainly

been enough time for Matt to follow Selene and then return to Avalon.

"The Avalon police didn't ask for Matt's cell phone info because he supposedly forgot it at home that night," he said, recalling the information they'd provided from their case file. He pulled up the report on Matt, which confirmed that his phone had been in Avalon the entire night.

"Too convenient," Rhea said, and the police chief echoed her comment.

"The kind of thing someone does if they don't want to be tracked," he said.

"But his Jeep has a navigation system," Rhea reminded them, only Jackson shook his head.

"Most NAV systems use a positioning system that's only a one-way stream of data. But if he has something with a cellular connection, that provider might have that info. It's something we'll have to investigate further if this info doesn't pan out," he said and went back to the data on the screen.

"It looks like Selene stopped for gas right before she got to Regina," he said.

"Just like we thought, since she left her house in a rush," Rhea said, recalling their conversation of the day before.

"That's our next stop. We'll see who was working that night and reach out to them." Jackson moved on to the next stop that the cell phone company engineer had identified.

"She was at the pub for a good half an hour. Probably to get dinner," Jackson said and frowned. "Not the best place for a woman alone."

"Not unless she's looking for a hookup. That is what you call it now, right?" the police chief said and glanced toward Rhea. "Sorry, ma'am. No offense intended."

"None taken, but Selene isn't that kind of woman. It makes me wonder why she would have stopped there."

The police chief snapped his fingers and screwed his eyes upward, as if searching for something at the tip of his memory. "Isn't the guy who owns that gas station buddies with the pub owners?"

Jackson searched his memory. "I think you're right, Bill. They may even be related. Cousins, I think."

"If the cousin was working he might suggest the pub if someone asks for a recommendation," Rhea added to the discussion.

"Or he may tell his employees to suggest the pub," the chief said. With a smile and a point of his finger at Jackson, he added, "Good work, Jax. Just remember what we discussed."

With that, the chief pivoted and marched out of the room, leaving Rhea with a puzzled look on her face. Her eyes narrowed and settled on him, clearly expecting an explanation.

He hesitated, but Rhea deserved to know. "Nothing that embarrasses us or the Avalon PD."

"And what if it does that? Are you willing to bury the investigation—"

"Have I done anything that would make you think that?" he challenged, a wildfire of anger rushing through him.

Demurely, seemingly chastised, she said in a soft tone, "No. You haven't."

"I made you a promise and I intend to keep it, Rhea. If you don't trust me—"

"I do, Jax. I'm sorry that I suggested otherwise. It's just...emotional for me, and I can't be as objective as I should."

"Neither can I, Rhea. You make me feel..." He jammed his hands on his hips and sucked in a breath. "We've finally got a solid lead and we need to keep our focus on this." He circled the pub on the map with the laser pointer and then moved it to a location by the lake, the last spot on Selene's journey.

Subdued, head slightly bowed, Rhea said, "I guess we hit the road to talk to some people."

"We do. Are you ready?" The words seemed simple enough, but they were filled with many more questions. Was she ready to learn more about that night? Ready for possibly more disappointment?

So many questions, but at least now they had the data to continue to ask those questions. *Thanks to Rhea*, he thought.

She met his gaze directly, her chin tilted defiantly. A tight smile on her face. "I'm ready."

Chapter Fifteen

The gas station was a no-frills no-name location that survived due to a lack of competition. For anyone who had underestimated the distance to either Denver or any of the ski resorts to the west, the gas station was a last resort.

Jackson parked in front of the tiny market the station boasted. *A patron can pick up some sodas or snacks, in addition to the gasoline*, Rhea thought. The far side of the station housed several mechanic's bays. As they stepped out of the car, a large mountain of a man clothed in grease-stained overalls ambled out of one of the bays. He wiped his hands with a cloth that wasn't much cleaner and frowned as he saw Jackson.

"Detective," he said when he approached, but didn't hold his hand out. Instead, he held them up to show they were just too dirty for a handshake.

"Hannibal. Good to see you. How's it going?" Jackson asked, totally at ease despite the hostile vibes she was sensing from the man.

"Got work and customers, but I don't think

you're here to talk about that," the man said. His voice was deep and with his longish brown hair and beard and large size, he reminded her of a bear, but not the cuddly type. The kind with sharp claws and teeth to tear you apart.

Jackson held his hands up as if in surrender. "Not here to create any problems. Just to ask a few questions."

Hannibal shrugged. "Ask away. I've got nothing to hide."

Which was just what she would expect someone to say if they did have something to hide.

"This is Rhea. Her twin sister, Selene, disappeared about six months ago, and we've got info that says she stopped here for gas," Jackson said.

A careless shrug of Hannibal's wide, thick shoulders was followed by, "I get lots of people stopping here for gas. I'd have remembered a looker like that." His stare in her direction, very much a leer, left Rhea feeling dirty.

"Watch it, Hannibal," Jackson warned. "Do you work the night shift?"

Hannibal shook his head. "Too old for that. Couple of local kids work the late shifts."

Jackson nodded. "What about the pub? Doesn't your brother own it?" he asked, puzzling Rhea, since she thought Jackson had said it was a cousin.

With another shake of his head and wipe of his

hands with the dirty cloth, Hannibal said, "My cousin Drew, but he doesn't do that at the pub."

Do what? she wondered at the same time as Jackson asked the question.

"Girls. Slavery. That kind of stuff," Hannibal answered, sending a shiver of fear through Rhea. While she hoped Selene was still alive, the thought of her having been trafficked…

"If someone asked for a recommendation for a restaurant—" Jackson began, but Hannibal quickly cut him off.

"I'd recommend the pub. Tell my boys to do the same. Family sticks together."

Jackson paused, but then challenged Hannibal. "Does family stick together enough to hide a murder? Or a kidnapping?"

The other man obviously didn't like the insinuation. "We're done here, Detective. You want to talk to me or my boys again, call my lawyer." Without missing a beat, the man walked away and back to the mechanic's bay. A second later, the sound of metal striking metal told them he was back at work.

Jackson peered at her. "Time to hit the pub."

THE OUTSIDE OF the pub was not quite what she expected for a place of supposedly ill repute. The parking lot and grounds surrounding the building were clean and the landscaping welcomed with colorful flowers and neat bushes. The cedar shake siding, trim and doors had a fresh coat of paint.

When they entered there were very few patrons, but a couple of people were eating a late breakfast. The biggest feature in the space was a large horseshoe bar that separated the dining area from a section boasting cocktail-height tables, a dance floor and an upraised stage.

The place smelled faintly of yeasty beer, fried eggs and bacon, with a lingering hint of disinfectant, as if the floors and other areas had just been cleaned.

They had no sooner entered when a thirty-something bearded man approached, a broad smile on his face. He stuck his hand out to Jackson and said, "Jax, dude, how are you doing?"

Jackson took the man's hand and pulled him in for a bro hug. "Marcus. What are you doing here?"

As the man stepped back from the embrace, he eyeballed Rhea and Jackson, as if to trying to figure out what they were doing together. "And you're…?"

She offered her hand to the man, and he shook it, politely and almost gently. "Rhea Reilly. Jackson and I are investigating my sister's disappearance."

Marcus lost a little of his earlier effusiveness and dipped his head respectfully. "Sorry to hear about that, but what brings you here?"

"We have some questions, Marcus. Is there somewhere—" Jackson peered all around the restaurant to see who might be listening "—more private."

Marcus nodded and swung his arm wide. "My office."

Marcus led the way, with Jackson and her following. As they walked, Jackson said, "Your office? You're working here?"

Marcus looked over his shoulder and shrugged. "After those fights you busted up last summer, the owner decided he needed to restore some law and order, so here I am."

Jackson explained for her. "Marcus used to be on the Regina police force, but decided to retire."

They had reached the door to a back office, and Marcus unlocked it. They followed him down a hall past storage areas and a kitchen to an office at the farthest end of the hall. As he sat and invited them to join him, Marcus said, "Let's be honest, Jax. I had an alcohol problem, but thanks to you I've been sober for over a year and I have a new chance at life. I've been the manager since last September."

"I'm glad to hear that, but isn't it hard for you to work here?" Jackson asked and held his hands wide in emphasis.

A quick, tense shrug answered him. "Not easy at times, but this was a great opportunity, and it's been working as you may have noticed."

Jackson nodded. "Haven't been called out here for anything major."

"Good. Let's hope it stays that way. So how can I help you with your investigation?" Marcus leaned back in his chair, which creaked with the motion.

Jackson glanced at her, and she understood. "My sister may have been here the night she disappeared. We're trying to figure out if she met anyone that night."

Marcus shared an uneasy glance with Jackson before blurting out, "We get lots of women here, especially on the weekends. They come in for fun. Maybe meet someone."

"Selene, Rhea's sister, probably just stopped for dinner. She wasn't here for more than about forty minutes," Jackson said.

Marcus raised a brow as if to say it didn't take long for what most women in the pub wanted, but he was gentleman enough not to say it. "I don't know how we can help with more."

Rhea pointed out his door to another office where she had noticed a number of monitors flashing images. "You have security cameras. Do you keep recordings from those cameras?"

Marcus leaned forward to track where she was pointing. He nodded and leaned back again, totally casual. "We do, but we only hold them for about two weeks. Unless there's some kind of incident. Then we label and store them."

"Would you possibly have any from November of last year? November 7, actually?" Jackson said.

Marcus immediately answered. "No, sorry."

"Are you sure?" Rhea asked, worried they were going to hit another dead end.

Marcus nodded. "I am. The PC for the recording system died on us right around then. Tech said it was toast and took it away. Set up a new system."

"Is it possible he still has that failed system?" Jackson asked.

"Possible," Marcus said and pulled open his desk drawer. He scrounged around, yanked out a wrinkled business card and handed it to Jackson. "Here's his info. I'll let him know you're coming."

"We truly appreciate that, Marcus. Thank you," Rhea said, grateful that the man hadn't been an obstructionist, which was what she'd been expecting after their earlier meeting with the gas station owner.

"My pleasure. Like I said before, we're trying to clean this place up, so anything to support our local police department," Marcus said as he rose and held his hand out to Jackson again. "I mean that, dude. You saved my life."

Jackson clasped the other man's hand in both of his. "I'm glad to see you're doing well, Marcus. Just remember we're all here for you."

"You always were. If you don't mind, I've got

some things to do before lunch," Marcus said and grimaced at the pile of papers on his desk.

"Totally get it and thanks again," Rhea said and hurried from the office to the restaurant, picturing Selene there. Wondering if someone had approached her. Someone who had decided to take her.

"Penny for your thoughts," Jackson said as they stepped outside and looked back at the pub. He smoothed a finger across the furrow in Rhea's forehead.

"Maybe something happened to her here. Someone who thought she was here for a hookup and decided to make that happen," Rhea said, worried that such an encounter may have turned into something violent.

"It's possible, Rhea. Although we've never had that kind of problem here," Jackson said.

Rhea crossed her arms and rubbed her hands up and down her arms. He hugged her close, offering comfort. Aware that, little by little, Rhea might be losing hope that Selene was still alive.

"Let's hit the road and see the tech."

The silence as they drove to the tech's offices weighed on him heavily, because Rhea was hurting. Luckily the office was just a block off Main Street and, as promised, Marcus had called ahead. The tech greeted them with no hesitation.

"Marcus says you want to look at their old system. I pulled it off the scrap pile for you."

The tech walked to a large worktable in his back room. A computer tower sat there, a little dusty and worse for wear.

Jackson scrutinized it and then peered at the tech. "No chance of it working?"

The tech shook his head. "Tried, but there was a head crash. Head plinked around that disk like a marble in a pinball machine," he said and mimicked something bouncing around with his fingers. "That's why it was on the scrap pile. I keep the older units around in case I need power supplies, motherboards. That kind of thing."

"Mind if we take it?" Jackson said, earning a puzzled look from Rhea, and he explained, "My cousins in Miami are tech savants. Maybe they can get something off the unit."

"I'd be happy to pull the drive for you," the tech said and went into action, removing it from the system and packing it up.

"Good luck with it," the young man said and handed the box to Jackson.

"Thanks for all your help," Rhea offered, and Jackson echoed her sentiments.

"We appreciate the assistance."

Outside the tech's office, Jackson paused by his cruiser and whipped out his cell phone, wasting no time to call his cousins. Robert answered on the first ring. "Cuz, long time no hear," he said.

"Sorry, Robbie. I've just been a little busy. How are you and Sophie doing?"

"We're doing well. Let me put you on speaker," Robbie said and, a second later, the tone grew a little tinny as the speaker kicked in.

"I'm putting you on speaker also, Robbie. I have Rhea Reilly on the line with me. We're working on a case together."

"Hi, Robbie. Sophie," Rhea said.

"Nice to meet you," Sophie said. "What can we help you with?"

"You always cut to the chase, Sophie," Jackson teased and plowed on. "We have a hard drive with a head crash that may have information we need."

Robbie let out a low whistle. "Head crash is bad, man. That head hitting the disk probably took out some data."

"Some, but not all I gather," Jackson said, feeling optimistic that if anyone could get information from the disk it would be his cousins.

"Not all. Can you send it to us?" Sophie said.

"We can courier it to you for morning delivery," Jackson said, and his cousins clearly understood.

"We'll work on it immediately. Anything in particular?" Robbie asked.

"The hard drive was on a security system. We're looking for camera images from November 7. Anything from about 7:30 p.m. to 9:00 p.m.," he said.

"We're on it, Jax. If we can't get it for you, no one can," Sophie said.

"Thank you. It means a lot to me, since it may help us find out what happened to my sister," Rhea said.

"Family is important. Remember that, Jax," Robbie said, guilt heavy in his tone.

Miami was so not his style, but he understood. "I get it. When I have a vacation coming up I'll come visit my parents and swing by South Beach to see you."

"We'll hold you to that, Jax," Sophie said, and then the line went dead.

Rhea narrowed her eyes and glanced at him. "Somehow I can't picture you in South Beach."

Jackson sighed. "A little too city, hot and humid for me, but my parents have a place not far from there, and my uncle married into a Cuban family in Miami."

"And your cousins are there?" Rhea asked.

Jackson nodded. "Robbie and Sophie have their own tech company that develops apps and software, but my aunt's family has this high-powered private investigation and security company. The Liberty Agency. Robbie and Sophie often help them."

"I guess law enforcement runs in the family," Rhea said as Jackson opened the door to the cruiser.

Jackson slipped back into the driver's seat and, as he did so, he said, "And the military. Several of the members of the Gonzalez family that runs the Liberty Agency also served. Plus my Aunt Mercedes and Uncle Robert work for the NSA in D.C."

"Wow. Super-secret shadowy types," she teased.

He was about to start the car when a chirp announced he had a text message. With a quick look, he said, "Declan sent the photos of the bonfire." He held the phone so she could see the first photo. But as they swiped from one to the other, it was clear that the results of their experiment were not close to the crime scene photos of Matt's bonfire.

"There's a lot of dark residue and...bones," Rhea said with a frown.

Jackson nodded. "The experts pretty much told me to expect the residue from the body tissues."

With a rough breath, Rhea said, "I guess the cremation theory is out, isn't it?"

Jackson laid a hand on her shoulder and squeezed. "Tabled for now. Once we get this package off to my cousins, there's not much for us to do. Maybe review the materials again? Call Avalon PD for updates."

RHEA WASN'T SURE she could spend another night looking at the information and worrying about being disappointed or whether whoever was after her would try something else.

"I'd like to take the night off and return to

Denver. Check in at my shop and maybe just get away from…everything," she said, and at his crestfallen face, she realized he'd interpreted it to include him. Speedily she added, "You're welcome to come with."

Peering at her, gray eyes squinted, awakening lines at the corners, he said, "It makes sense, because I want to make sure you're okay, but are you sure?"

She was and wasn't and hated that she couldn't figure out what she wanted with him. She punted and said, "You can use my guest room. Selene normally stays there."

He hesitated, but then nodded. "Let's get this package mailed and swing by my house to get our things."

"Sure," she said and sat there, anticipating what it would feel like to have him in her home. He was so big and masculine. Country. Her apartment was a lot like her. Artsy. Feminine. City.

In no time, they had run to the courier service and dropped off the hard drive, as well as made the trip to his house to pick up things for an overnight stay in Denver. Jackson also changed out of his police uniform into street clothes, and her heart did a little jump at the sight of him. The faded jeans hugged his powerful legs and trim waist. A pale blue button-down shirt brought out shards of blue in his gray eyes. But a loose denim jacket barely hid the bulge that told her he was wearing his holster and service weapon.

As they drove, she stayed silent, her thoughts bouncing around like the marble in the pinball game the tech had mentioned earlier.

She hadn't really expected to be staying in Jackson's home and the time spent there with him had provided her a whole new view of the detective she had nearly barreled over just a few days ago. He was a man who loved his family and obviously wanted one of his own, judging from the home he had built himself. He was honorable, even if it might cost him personally. And a leader, judging from the way Diego, Declan and even Marcus had assisted with the investigation. They clearly respected him, but he obviously cared about them, as well.

She was so lost in her thoughts that she hadn't realized they had entered the city limits until Jackson parked. They did the short walk to her building and she guided him toward the elevator at the back of the lobby. "I'm on the top floor."

Jackson took the time to appreciate Rhea's building. It was done in art deco style, with speckled black terrazzo floors and marbled walls. Sconces and other accents in shiny steel lightened all those dark colors as did the ornate wooden doors of the elevator.

As they stepped into the elevator, Rhea stuck a key into the panel to unlock the penthouse access and once they reached that floor, the elevator opened right into her home. A very feminine home filled with neutral-colored furniture with plush cushions and brightly colored accent pillows. The walls boasted an assortment of artwork, including some of Rhea's pieces. He recognized them immediately based on what he'd seen on her website. The paintings had that passion and life that jumped off the walls and called to him to take a closer look.

"Do you like?" she asked, hands clasped before her. A nervous seesaw from side to side while she waited for his opinion.

"I love it. You make the image come alive," he said and smiled. He turned and held his hands wide. "This is very nice. Full of life. Color."

"Thank you. It's taken some time to get it here, but I'm happy with it," she said and visibly relaxed, holding out a hand to him, which he took in his.

"I can see why. I know it's early, but how about a walk and dinner?" he said, splaying a hand across his stomach to hide the hunger grumble he felt building inside.

"I'd like that. One of my favorite places is just a few blocks away."

"I want to get to know what you like. How you live." She had intrigued him on multiple levels, from her determination and work on her sister's case, to her strength while in harm's way and the art on the walls that spoke of her passion for life. And, of course, the steel hidden beneath her delicate exterior that said she was the kind of woman he could have by his side. A woman who didn't wilt when faced with adversity.

"Great. I think you'll really like it." She tugged on his hand gently to steer him toward the door. He went willingly, eager for Rhea to have a distraction from her sister's case and the attacks against her, if only for the one night. Eager to get know more about her and how she lived.

Outside, they hurried away from the mall area and toward the Larimer Square historic district with its heritage buildings, eclectic shops and restaurants. With the warmer weather a number of the restaurants had created al fresco dining areas on the sidewalks. Edison lights had been strung overhead and across the street, creating a festive feel especially when combined with vibrant banners touting an upcoming music festival. Beneath trees boasting bright spring green leaves rested planters with vibrant blooms and small bushes that softened the urban feel of the buildings.

Rhea dragged him to the entrance to a steak place and, at his questioning look, she said, "I love a good piece of beef as much as you do."

He swung her arm playfully. "I'd tell you I'm vegan, but you already saw me chow down at Deck's."

"I did, and I hope you'll love this place also,"

she said, and with another tug, urged him into the restaurant.

The host at the podium, a youngish man in his late twenties, raised an eyebrow as Rhea came in with Jackson. The man swung around the podium to give her an effusive hug. "Rhea! So good to see you! And who's this?" he asked, shooting a warning glare in Jackson's direction.

With a playful shove, she pushed the host away. "Easy, Randy. This is Detective Whitaker. He's helping me with Selene's case."

Jackson shook the other's man hand and tried not to be too stung that Rhea hadn't said he was a friend. But then again, he wouldn't be too happy about being friend-zoned, either, since he wanted more from her.

"Your favorite table is free," Randy said, grabbed some menus and guided them to a spot right by the windows where they could have dinner and people watch, as well.

After they were seated, Jackson leaned close and over the top of his menu whispered, "If you and Randy—"

Rhea chuckled and skimmed her hand across his forearm. "He's just a friend. A friend who's probably way more interested in you than me."

Jackson peered at the man, who smiled at him.

"Oh, okay. I was worried he might think I was competition or something."

Rhea smiled, and it was the smile of a seductress. Her crystal blue gaze darkened and her voice was husky, sexy, as she said, "No one can compete with you, Jax."

Wow, definitely not friend-zoned. "I can say the same about you, Rhea. My one wish is that we hadn't met the way we did, but I'm glad we've met."

"Me, too," she said and set her menu down.

The waiter approached at that moment and said. "Good to see you again, Rhea. The usual?"

"The usual, Sam," she answered and handed him the menu.

"What about you, sir?" the waiter said, his tone not anywhere near as friendly, warning that Rhea had another possible protector.

"The porterhouse. Medium rare," he said. As the waiter rushed away to place their orders, Jackson picked up his water glass and glanced at her over the rim. "You have a lot of defenders."

Rhea grinned and shook her head. "They're just not used to me bringing a man here," she said and then covered her mouth. He thought he heard her mutter, "Stupid, stupid, stupid." It brought a smile to his face, since it made him special and since it confirmed that Rhea lacked guile.

He took hold of her hand. "I'm glad I'm special. I am special, right?"

With a chuckle, she twined her fingers with his. "And dense, if you don't know that yet."

Sam, the waiter, returned with a wine bottle

and made quite a show of opening it. "Courtesy of Randy. One of our best cabernets."

They both offered their thanks, and Jackson took the first sip. "Excellent."

Sam filled their glasses and walked away to give them privacy. Jackson raised his glass and toasted. "To friendship."

She tapped her glass to his and surprised him again with her boldness. "To friendship and more, Jax."

With a dip of his head, he said, "To more."

Chapter Sixteen

Jackson lounged on Rhea's sofa, his muscled arms resting along the top of the cushions. He'd taken off his denim jacket and carefully folded it to cradle the holster he also removed. The pile of the jacket and holster sat off to the side, a very masculine contrast to the brightly colored pillows tucked all around him.

Her belly was full with the fabulous filet mignon and wine she'd had for dinner, as well as the cheesecake slice she'd shared with Jackson. In truth, she was a little sleepy and, dare she say it, at peace for the first time in months.

Hard to believe, considering she still didn't know what had happened to Selene and someone was trying to either kill her or drive her off the investigation.

But with Jackson there…

So many different emotions raced through her in addition to the peace. Comfort. Need, especially as he settled his gaze on her. His gray eyes were dark, almost black as he invited her to join him on the couch. Invited her to more.

She didn't hesitate, taking hold of his hand and snuggling into his side, her head pillowed against his chest. His heartbeat loud and beginning to race beneath her ear.

He skimmed his hand across her hair, smoothing it. Slipping beneath the hair at her shoulders to her neck, where he massaged her muscles and then shifted his hand downward again to hug her close.

She snuggled in tighter and higher, until her lips were barely inches from his. Laying her hand on his chest, she pressed upward to trace the edge of his jaw with her mouth. Beneath her hand, his muscles tensed.

She looked up at him. Found the question in his gaze. "I'm sure, Jax. I've never been more sure of anything in my life."

Her words released his control. Urgently he slipped his hands to her waist and urged her upward. Their first tentative kiss, one of invitation and acceptance, quickly flared into one of heat and passion. They kissed over and over, mouths meeting ruthlessly, hungrily.

As Jackson brought his hand around to cup her breast, she moaned and moved to straddle his thighs. His body was hard everywhere. Strong. So strong and insistent against hers.

She shifted on him, needing him. Needing to

release her control and savor what this amazing man could provide.

Jackson groaned as Rhea moved on him. He clasped her hips with his hands and urged her to still. "Rhea. Are you sure?"

"Yes, I am. Come with me." She eased from his lap and tugged him off the sofa.

He willingly followed, needing Rhea like he had no other woman. Wanting to explore the complex woman he'd only known for a few days. Humbled that he could feel so much for her in so short a time.

In her bedroom, she went straight to the bed and offered him a smile that was both welcoming and hesitant. He bent and tasted that smile. Accepted the invitation and hoped to ease her sudden reluctance, because if he couldn't...

He wouldn't pressure her.

He turned to sit on the bed, bringing her face-to-face with him.

Cupping her cheek, he gentled her and welcomed her into the V of his outspread legs. Gently he strummed his thumb across her cheek. Soothed his other hand up and down her side.

She laid her hands on his shoulders before leaning close and kissing him again. The kiss tentative at first until passion ignited need so intense, it was impossible to stop.

Kissing was interrupted only to remove clothes until flesh was against flesh, and Jackson slipped

on protection. He covered her with his body, joining with her. Breaths caught with the union. Exploded as Jackson moved within her, pulling her
ever higher. Pushing them closer and closer to
the edge until, with a final thrust, they tumbled
over the edge together.

Rhea cuddled tight to Jackson's side, her thigh
tossed over his. Her head pillowed on his muscled
chest. He draped his arm down her back, holding
her near. He laid his other arm across hers, pin-
ning it against his chest. His touch soothing as
he grazed his hand along her upper arm.

"That was...nice," she said, unable to find the
right word to describe what she was feeling. Satisfied. Peaceful. Expectant.

"Ouch. Just nice," he teased, laughter in his
tone and in the shake of his body beneath hers.

She leaned an elbow on his chest and glanced
up at him. "Okay, maybe more than nice. But
don't let your ego get out of hand."

He inched a dark brow upward. "A lot more
than nice?"

Chuckling, she settled back onto his chest and
drifted her hand down his midsection and lower.
"Maybe. Want to try for way more than nice?"

He rolled her beneath him. "Definitely."

THEY WERE HEADING back to Rhea's apartment
after visiting her gallery the next morning when
the call came from his cousin Sophie.

"I hope this is good news," Jackson said as he answered and paused by the entrance to the building.

"So nice to talk to you, too, *primo*," Sophie teased.

"Sorry, cuz. It is nice to hear from you. How are you?" he said and looked in Rhea's direction. With a dip of his head, he confirmed it was the call for which they'd been waiting.

"I'm fine, and so are you. Robbie and I managed to get some images off the hard drive of that woman whose photo you sent. It wasn't easy. We had to get the corrupted data off the drive, rebuild the FAT table and—"

"Sophie, English please," he said, teasing her about the geek speak.

Sophie chuckled and said, "I'm sending the photos via email, and I'll text them to you, as well." He heard the click-clack of keys to confirm the dispatch of the images.

"I owe you big time."

"You do, so how about you come visit and bring your lady friend, as well?" Sophie said, laying on the guilt.

"My mom told you to say that, didn't she?"

Sophie's husky laugh confirmed it. "Call us if you need anything else, *primo*."

"I will, Sophie. Thank Robbie for me," he said and hung up to peer at the images she had sent.

Jackson angled the phone so Rhea could see

the grainy black-and-white photos. The first was of Selene inside the pub, sitting and eating. There were other patrons nearby, including two heavily bearded and long-haired men who seemed to be looking in Selene's direction. The second photo was similar to the first, but in this one there was no doubt that the men were staring at Rhea's sister. The last three images were from the exterior of the pub. Selene near her car and, after, another one showing her pulling away, but in the background, the two bearded men again. They were leaning against what looked like a Jeep. The final photo created a blast of memories through Jackson's brain.

The Jeep was backing out, providing a glimpse of its front bumper.

It was that bumper that had piqued his interest, since it was way too similar to what he'd seen only moments before they'd been rammed and almost driven into the back of the logging truck.

"Is that—"

"The SUV that hit us? I think it might be," he said and used his thumb and forefinger to zoom the photo and enlarge the bumper section.

"A definite maybe," he said.

Rhea wiggled her forefinger at the phone. "Go back to the earlier images. I think I've seen that man before."

He did as she asked, and she nodded. "He was

in the police station when I came to speak to the chief."

Jackson zoomed the image to focus on the faces of the two men. Their heavy beards and long hair hid many of their features, but there were some similarities in the shapes of their eyes, noses and lips. "They could be brothers," he said, tracing those features with his forefinger.

"They could be. And I had a witness who said she drove by and noticed another Jeep by Selene's car that night. We've been thinking that it was Matt's Jeep, but maybe it wasn't. Maybe it was this Jeep."

"There's only one way to find out. You have contact info for that witness, don't you?"

Rhea nodded and skimmed through the info on her phone. "I do. I guess we go see her."

"We do, only..." He wanted to tell her not to get her hopes up, but that would be unrealistic. The photos and connection to their attackers was beyond coincidence. It was a solid lead, and one they had to follow.

"Let's go," he said and held his hand out to her.

Her smile was grim as she slipped her hand into his. "I'm ready. Let's go."

GAIL FRAZIER WAS a sixtysomething LPN who worked at an assisted living facility in Regina and volunteered with an organization that provided meals and companionship to seniors. She had been coming home from one of those volunteer assignments when she had seen Selene's car and the unidentified SUV.

"What time do you think you left Mrs. Wilson's home?" Jackson asked as they sat with the LPN in her workplace's cafeteria.

"Much later than normal. Mrs. Wilson was a little despondent that day since it was her husband's birthday. He passed several years ago," Gail explained.

Rhea nodded. "That was so nice that you stayed to cheer her up."

Gail sniffled, and her eyes filled with tears. "I lost my own husband two years ago and started volunteering to fill the empty hours. My assignments help me as much as I help them," she said and picked up her coffee mug that said "#1 Nurse." She took a sip and after said, "I think I was there until about nine. Maybe a little earlier. I got Mrs. Wilson settled in bed, cleaned up a bit and then drove home. That's when I saw the cars by the lake."

Jackson pulled out a photo of Selene's sedan. He laid it in front of Gail. "Is this the car you saw that night?"

Gail nodded, her head shifting up and down emphatically. "I think so. I didn't think anything about it that night since people stop to look at the lake at all hours."

"What made you reach out to me and not the police?" Rhea asked.

Gail shrugged and pointed to the photo. "At first I didn't think it was unusual. But then I ran across your posts on Facebook asking for any additional information. It got me thinking about that night."

Jackson considered the older woman, judging her sincerity. "So you suddenly remembered a second car months later."

Another emphatic nod answered him. "I did. I wish I had made the connection earlier, but I didn't. Like I said, nothing seemed off until I saw Rhea's post and started thinking about it."

Which would make her testimony in court totally vulnerable to challenge. Any good defense lawyer would chip away at it to attempt to prove she imagined the second car as a way to help Rhea. She was a caregiver by nature and liked to volunteer to help others. Giving Rhea that info totally fit her nature, even if the veracity of the information might be doubtful.

Jackson tried to push her some more. "You thought the other car by the lake was a Jeep. One like this?" He slipped a photo of Matt's Wrangler in front of the LPN.

She laid her hand on the photo and drew it near for a closer inspection. With a shrug and a small frown, she said, "Like this one, but not this new or nice. The one I saw looked older. More beat-up."

Jackson shared a look with Rhea. If Gail was right, Matt was moving further down on the suspect list with each new bit of information they gathered. Opening his folder, he drew out a photo that his cousins had provided. "What about this SUV?"

Gail peered at the photo, squinting at the image. She picked up the glasses hanging on a bejeweled chain around her neck. Slipping on the cheaters, she said, "I don't really need them, but use them just to be sure of the directions on some of the patients' medications. The print is just too small and this photo... Well, it's quite grainy."

With the cheaters in place, she perused the photo for a too-long minute before she set it down and gestured to it. "Like that one."

Rhea leaned toward the other woman and placed her hand on the photo. "Like that one? So you don't think this is the SUV you saw?"

Gail got snippy. "I didn't say that, did I, young lady?"

Rhea inhaled deeply, held her breath and then in a gentler tone said, "I'm sorry, Gail. I truly appreciate that you came forward so we can find out what happened to Selene."

Seemingly chastened by Rhea's statement, Gail picked up the photo once again and reexamined it. When she set it down, she said, "I think this was the car. I remember it having that weird bumper thing."

The same weird bumper thing that I saw just before we were rammed, Jackson thought.

"That's important, Gail. Thank you," Rhea said and shot Jackson a look, as if saying, *Tag, it's your turn*.

He ran with it. "Did you see anyone near the cars? Selene? Anyone else?"

She shook her head. "Just the cars. I didn't think to look at the lakeshore. Like I said, it didn't seem anything was out of the ordinary and truth be told, I was tired. I just wanted to get home and get some rest."

"We understand. You do hard work here and with the volunteering... You must be exhausted late at night." Rhea laid a hand on Gail's, offering her thanks with the touch.

"I am, but like I said before, it helps me, as well. If there's anything I can do, please let me know," Gail said and glanced at her watch. "I really should get back to my patients. It'll be lunchtime soon and I have to get their medications ready."

When she rose from her chair, Jackson and Rhea did the same. Jackson shook her hand and said, "We appreciate the time you took. If need be, would you be willing to testify to what you saw?"

Gail peered at Rhea and said, "I would and

I'm so sorry for your loss. It must be difficult for you."

Rhea's lips were in a tight line, her voice choked with emotion as she said, "Thank you again, Gail. I appreciate you coming forward. It's been truly helpful."

With a quick nod, Gail slipped away to return to her patients, and Jackson and Rhea left the facility. At the cruiser, Jackson crossed his arms and leaned against the fender, facing Rhea. She stood before him, arms wrapped around herself defensively. "I know this is upsetting."

Rhea shook her head and her dangling silver earrings danced against her neck. "It is, but I can deal."

"Can you deal with the possibility Matt wasn't the one who killed Selene?" Jackson pressed, hating to hurt her, but needing her to acknowledge he was likely not their suspect any longer.

"She's not dead," Rhea said, which shouldn't have surprised him, but it did.

"Rhea, please," he urged and reached for her, but she brushed off his touch and stepped away from him.

Chin tilted up and ice in her crystal blue gaze, she said, "If we've eliminated Matt, then we move on to the other scenarios, and they include the possibility that Selene is alive, Detective. So what do we do next?"

Chapter Seventeen

Ugh, detective-zoned. Far worse than friend-zoned, but he understood that Gail's information had upended what had been the most plausible explanation for what had happened to Selene. The others, including that Selene was alive…

He pushed off the bumper and opened the door for her. Meeting her gaze, he said, "We head back to the pub and speak to Marcus. Maybe he knows more about those two men."

Without waiting for her reply, he walked around and eased into the driver's seat. They were at the pub in no time. Quite a number of vehicles were in the parking lot, since it was almost lunch hour. Jackson parked, and Rhea and he entered. They located Marcus, who once again took them into his office to avoid prying eyes and gossip about Jackson's visit.

"How can I help you again?" Marcus asked with a tired sigh as he plopped into his chair.

"Rough morning?" Jackson asked, inching a brow upward in emphasis.

"Totally, dude. One of the chefs burned himself pretty bad, and we had a problem with one of the freezers, but I'm handling it," Marcus advised and skimmed his gaze from Rhea to him and back.

"You two look like your morning was as bad," Marcus said.

"You could say that," Rhea blurted out.

Marcus trained his gaze on Jackson, as if asking for his confirmation. Instead, Jackson took the photos from his folder and handed them to his former colleague. "What can you tell us about those two?"

Marcus shuffled through the photos and then gestured to Rhea with them. "This is your sister in the photos?"

Rhea nodded. "It is."

Marcus let out a low whistle. "You really are identical, aren't you?"

"Marcus, focus," Jackson said, and it brought back memories of working with the other man on the force. Although he'd been a good cop, he'd also been easily distracted.

"Easy, dude," Marcus warned and glanced at the photos again before handing them back to Jackson. Fingers laced, he laid his hands across his midsection and said, "They apparently come in every few months."

"Have you seen them lately?" Jackson asked.

Marcus tilted his head to the side and looked

upward, searching his memory, and then shook his head. "Come to think of it, no. The staff calls them the 'Mountain Men.'"

Rhea jumped in with, "Why is that?"

With a shrug, Marcus said, "When they first came in, I got bad vibes. I asked the old-timers who gave me the skinny on them. That they seemed like recluses who only came down every few months. Kept to themselves. Creeped out some of the female customers."

"In what way?" Rhea asked, her gaze narrowed as she trained it on Marcus.

"I'm told they'd stare at them. Make comments. I wasn't around at the time, but they were asked to leave one night and got in the old manager's face. Pushed him around."

"Did you call the police? Is there a report possibly?" Jackson said, hoping that there would be so they might identify the men.

Marcus shook his head. "Sorry, but they didn't. It got handled, and no one was hurt."

"Do you mind if we ask your staff about them?" Jackson said.

Marcus frowned. "Dude, we're just about to start the lunch service. Can I send them to the station later?"

He glanced in Rhea's direction. She was bouncing her feet nervously, expectantly. She clearly would prefer to deal with it now as he would, but Marcus had been open and helpful, and he didn't want to push. Besides, they had things to do at the station anyway.

"We'll be there," he said, earning a quick hard glance from Rhea, but she remained silent.

"I appreciate that, Jax. I'll speak to my guys and ask them to go over after their shift. I'll make a list of who might have info also, just in case." Marcus stood as if to reinforce it was time for them to go.

"Just in case?" Rhea asked and stood, her face puzzled.

Marcus did a quick shrug. "Some of my guys… Let's just say they're not fans of the police. But I'll get them to you, I promise."

"Appreciate the help, Marcus. We truly do," Jackson said.

Once they were out in the restaurant, Jackson played it up as if to make it seem like their visit had been only a friendly one, since several eyes had turned in their direction. "Thanks for that donation to the PAL fund, Marcus. We truly appreciate it," he said, his voice loud enough to be overheard by those in the area.

Marcus smiled and chuckled. "You're welcome, Jax. Anything for a friend."

Rhea went up on tiptoes and brushed a kiss across his cheek, truly grateful for his assistance. "Thank you."

With a wink and a broad smile, Marcus said, "Anything for you, pretty lady."

Rhea returned the grin and suddenly felt the possessive press of Jackson's hand at the small of her back. Still angry, she glared at him and pushed away, eager to return to the police station. As she had told Jackson earlier, she thought she had seen one of the men at the station.

She hurried from the pub, the soft soles of her espadrilles creating a dull thud with each quick step. She shoved through the door to the cruiser and didn't wait for Jackson to do the gentlemanly thing. Grabbing the handle, she waited for the *kerthunk* to signal that he'd opened the lock, but when it didn't happen immediately, she turned to find him standing there.

"What?" she asked, wondering at his delay.

"I know you're angry," he began, but she shut him down with a sharp raise of a brow and the crossing of her arms. She lifted her face to stare at his, her chin tilted in defiance.

"My possibility is as plausible as any that remain."

Jackson jammed his hand on his hips, looked away from her penetrating gaze and sucked in deep breath. Blowing it out sharply, he said, "It is, Rhea. But it's the one that will bring you the most pain if it proves false. I don't want you to experience that kind of pain. Again."

His words mollified her anger, filled as they were with concern. "I'm a big girl, Jax. While it may be painful if I'm wrong, it brings me comfort to think she might be out there somewhere. To think we might be able to save her from suffering if she's alive."

He nodded, and while she sensed he had more to say, he bit his tongue. Literally, because she could swear she saw him wince before he unlocked the doors and walked around to his side of the cruiser.

She eased into her seat and buckled up, and Jackson took off for the police station. The trip was short, since Regina wasn't all that big. As they crossed Main Street, its beauty struck her once again and made her itch to finish the sketch she'd started the other day. When her gaze skimmed to Jackson, the sharp lines of his handsome face stole her breath and roused passion, both to finish his sketch and to be with him again.

At the station house, the desk sergeant who had been on duty the day Rhea had first come to see the chief was guarding the entrance again. Rhea smiled at her, and at the dip of Jackson's head, she buzzed them through.

But Jackson paused right past the barrier and turned to Rhea. "Do you see the officer here who had brought in one of our possible suspects?"

Rhea gazed around the various desks, looking for the middle-aged officer she thought she had seen with someone who looked like one of the Mountain Men, but she didn't spot him. But then two officers emerged with coffee from what must have been a break room. She pointed in their direction. "I think that's him. The one to the left."

Jackson nodded and called out to his colleague. "Officer Bellevue. Do you have a moment for us?"

The officer hurried over. "How can I help?" he said as he shook Rhea's hand and dipped his head in Jackson's direction.

Jackson opened his folder and handed a photo to Officer Bellevue. "Have you seen either of these men before?"

The man examined it and tapped on the face of one of the men. "Had this one in earlier this week."

Jackson shared a hopeful glance with Rhea. "Can you pull your report for us?"

A bright stain of color erupted across the officer's face. "I'm sorry, Jax, but I didn't file one. I brought him in for some minor shoplifting, but the owner said that if he paid for the items, she wouldn't press charges. He did, so I let him go with a warning."

Jackson dragged a hand through his hair in frustration. "You didn't get a name or address?"

"I did get a name, although it took some doing. Guy kept on muttering about how his brother would be so mad at him for getting in trouble. He did have a wallet, but no ID. " Officer Bellevue said and pulled a small notepad from his shirt pocket. Flipping through the pages, he stopped at one and said, "Wade Garrett."

"Thank you, officer. That's really helpful," Rhea said with a smile, trying to ease the officer's earlier upset about not filing a report.

"If you need me to run him down—"

Jackson held up a hand to stop the other man. "Thanks, but we'll do it. If there's anything else you can think of, please let us know."

"I will, Jax," he said and walked away to his desk.

"A name. I guess that's a start," Rhea said.

Since they'd almost made peace after that morning's upset, Jackson didn't want to tell her it wasn't much of a start, especially if the man had provided a fake name. "Let's go to my office, so we can try to track him down."

He laid a hand at her waist and was grateful she didn't shy away as she'd done before. With gentle pressure, he guided her to his office. Tossing the folder with the photos on his desk, he sat and explained to Rhea what he was doing on his computer. He couldn't let her see the screen once he logged on to the various police databases since she wasn't authorized, but he did turn the screen slightly as he added the photos his cousins had retrieved to their digital notebook and also updated the information from Gail Frazier.

"I'm going to run Wade Garrett through the state and federal databases to see if we get a hit," he said and moved the screen out of Rhea's line of sight.

"Do you think you will?" Rhea asked, worrying her lower lip, her look expectant as she leaned toward him, almost as if urging him to get going.

Jackson shrugged. "Maybe."

He tapped away on the keys while Rhea sat there, almost bouncing up and down in her chair. The records he searched brought up several hits in various court cases, but as he skimmed through the available details it became clear a few of the cases dated to the early 1940s and involved an adult male.

"Got a few hits involving criminal cases, but the person would be way too old," he said, but quickly added, "Although it could be a parent."

After reviewing the last few entries, he leaned back in his chair and said, "Nothing here, and in Colorado vital records are considered confidential and not online. Plus, that assumes they're locals, and we don't know that. I'll search the DMV records, even though Bellevue said he didn't have a license. It might mean he just didn't have it with him."

But the DMV search didn't produce any hits and he advised Rhea of that. "Since that was a bust, I'm going to search through the national criminal databases that are available."

"Like which ones?" Rhea asked, craning her

neck toward the screen, clearly wanting to be involved.

While Jackson entered his username and password into the first system, he said, "A whole alphabet soup of databases. NCIC. NICS."

A BRIGHT GRIN and chuckle relieved her earlier intensity. "Definitely alphabet soup. Which reminds me that we haven't had lunch yet." As if to reinforce her comment, her stomach grumbled noisily and she hastily laid a hand over her midsection to quiet the noise.

Jackson smiled and with a flip of his hand at the monitor, he said, "This may take a while. There are some chips and things in the break room, but also a nice sandwich shop just a few doors down on Main Street." He reached into this top desk drawer, found a take-out menu and handed it to her.

Rhea accepted the menu. The edges were ragged, and the paper was soft, as if it had been handled many times. "I guess you order from there a lot."

With a chagrined smile, Jackson said, "You have a lot of late nights in this job. Sandwiches make it easier to eat and work at the same time."

"But not healthier, mentally or physically. I'll take a walk and go get us something."

She placed the menu on his desktop, but as

she moved away, he raised an index finger. "No salad. I'm allergic to green things."

She chuckled as he had intended and shook her head. "Got it. No salad."

Hurrying out to the street, she walked toward the center of town, where most of the stores and restaurants were located. She remembered seeing one place that sold pot pies with various fillings. They'd be a nice hearty lunch and force Jackson to take a break from the tedium of searching through the databases.

The shop had quite an assortment of fillings, from one mimicking a Cuban sandwich to the more traditional chicken and turkey pot pie variations. She chose the chicken for herself, but a chili-style filling for Jackson.

She had barely gone a block when she got that feeling she was being followed. Turning quickly, she caught a glimpse of someone ducking into a small alley between two of the buildings.

The hackles rose down her neck and back, and she quickened her pace almost to a run. Turning every now and then to see if she was still being followed. She thought she caught another glimpse of someone as she hit the stairs for the police station, but safety was just a few steps away.

She stumbled on the last step, almost sending herself tumbling into the glass doors for the station, but she righted herself and managed not to drop their lunch while doing it.

Bursting through the doors, she immediately drew the attention of the desk sergeant who jumped to her feet, eyebrows knitted with worry. "Are you okay, Rhea?"

Rhea peered back over her shoulder. No one outside on the steps. Lifting her gaze to glance across the street, she thought she saw a big, bearded man again, one who looked too much like the one in the photos from the pub, but then he vanished.

Maybe it was all in her imagination. Her mother had told her on more than one occasion that she had a vivid imagination and, of course, it came part and parcel with being an artist.

"I'm okay. Just a little spooked."

The officer glanced past her and out the door, as well. "I'll buzz you through," she said after apparently determining that everything was in order.

"Thanks," she said and hurried to Jackson's door.

He was at work, but looked at her as she walked in. He was immediately in action, coming to her side to take the package and guide her into a chair.

As he wrapped his arm around her, she realized for the first time that she was shaking.

"What happened, Rhea? You look like you've seen a ghost," he said, drawing her closer and brushing a kiss across her temple.

She wiggled her head, embarrassed. "Nothing, only… I thought someone was following me."

Jackson muttered a curse. "I'm sorry. I should have told you that I had one of our officers trailing you to make sure you were safe."

"Maybe that's why I felt I was being followed," she said with a shrug, wanting to alleviate the obvious guilt he was feeling.

"Maybe," he said, hugged her hard again and skimmed another kiss on her cheek.

A rough, overly loud cough, drew them apart.

She peered over her shoulder to find Jackson's boss staring at them intently. His face as hard and rough as the stone outcroppings on the mountains around Regina.

"Am I interrupting something?" the chief said and arched one bushy gray eyebrow.

"I just had a scare," Rhea said and slid to one side of her chair to create some distance from Jackson.

The chief crooked a finger in Jackson's direction and he rose, then stepped outside his office to speak to his boss. Bodies tilted toward each other, voices low, the two men spoke and, while she was unable to hear, their posture and the few chest pokes the chief gave Jackson said it all. He was clearly not happy with what he had just seen.

When the other man left, Jackson laid his hands on his hips and looked upward before entering his office and shutting the door for privacy.

"He's angry, isn't he?" she said as Jackson busied himself with removing the pot pies and cutlery from the bag. He ripped the bag open and spread it across the surface of the desk to act like a place mat.

"Jackson, talk to me," she said and placed her hand on his forearm to still his angry motion.

"Chief says I need to wrap this up. We're wasting too many man hours and resources. I'm letting it get too personal." His words were clipped and chilly.

She laced her fingers together and laid her hands in her lap. Peering at them, she said, "I'm sorry, Jax. I know how important becoming chief is to you—"

"But not more important than justice, Rhea. We're close. I can feel it," he said.

His body was stiff, and he had clearly shut himself off from her, so she decided not to press. They ate in silence, and while the food may have been scrumptious, she didn't taste a thing thanks to the emotions roiling inside.

Jackson gobbled his pie down in record time and swung back to his computer. Barely a second later, he returned to his two-fingered pecking at the keyboard. His brow furrowed as he paused, probably to review the information on the screen. That process was repeated over and over while Rhea picked at her pot pie, keeping herself occupied with counting the peas and carrots as she ate to keep from bothering Jackson.

A good hour went by like that until Jackson blew out a rough breath and pushed away from the computer. He leaned his elbows on the arms of his chair and steepled his fingers before his mouth, clearly unhappy.

"Nothing, right?" she said, reading his signals.

He nodded, his frustration apparent despite his earlier optimism that they were close to finding something. "Nothing. Nada. Zilch. Zero."

She was about to say something, she didn't know what, when he slapped his hands on his desk and said, "But that's not stopping me. Us. I'll be right back."

He rushed from his office and came back with a large roll of paper. She quickly cleared off the remnants of their lunch and threw them away so Jackson could unfurl the paper across his desk. A map of Regina and the adjacent mountain areas. He jabbed at the mountains and said, "Marcus said that it seemed as if the men had come down from the mountain. What if they did? What if they live in one of these nearby areas?"

"But these are all protected lands, right?"

"That doesn't stop poachers or squatters." He traced his index finger along the highway that ran along the base of the mountain peaks and near the lake where Selene had last been seen.

"They could have grabbed her here." He jabbed

at the map by the lake. "And taken her somewhere on one of these mountains."

Rhea peered at the map. "That's a lot of territory to cover."

"For sure," Jackson said, but then grabbed his desk phone and tapped out a few numbers. "Dillon. Do you have a few minutes to help me?"

His smile confirmed Dillon would be over quickly, and within seconds, another officer was at Jackson's door. "You needed me, boss?"

Jackson nodded. "You're an expert hiker, aren't you?"

The other officer nodded and grinned. "I am. You need some advice on hiking trails?" he said and approached the desk. He barely looked old enough to be a cop, making her feel suddenly old, even though she was only twenty-eight.

Jackson gestured to the two mountains closest to Regina. "How hard would it be to hike up either of these peaks? Maybe even build yourself a little cabin. A private one."

Dillon let out a low whistle. "Depends on the time of year."

"Fall. November," Jackson said.

Dillon shot a quick glance in her direction and with a shrug said, "If there isn't snow on the ground, it's not so hard on this peak. There's actually a small road that goes up about halfway. You get some hikers who drive and then head to one of the lower peaks on foot. It takes more experienced climbers to actually reach the summit."

"So it gets enough traffic that it might be hard to hide?" Rhea asked. If she was trying to hide, she wouldn't want a lot of people traipsing nearby.

Dillon considered her comment and then nodded. "Enough traffic. Plus, there's a ski resort here," he said and gestured to the far side of the mountain, the area closest to where Selene disappeared.

Jackson stood, arms akimbo, perusing the map. He gestured to the other mountain. "What about this area?"

Dillon mimicked Jackson's pose and examined the map. With a nod of his head, he said, "That's a tougher hike for sure. Not many people do it."

"How would you get up there if you wanted to?" Rhea asked, leaning over to look at the map.

Dillon scratched his head. "Rumor has it there's an old logging trail, but it's been closed to the public for ages." He leaned his hands on the desk and shifted closer to the map, inspecting it more carefully. Running his finger along one stretch of highway, he said, "Somewhere around here."

"Satellite image might confirm it," Jackson said and hurried back to his computer. In no time, he had a map of the area up on the screen and turned it around so they could all see it. He zoomed in on the image and gestured to one section. "This looks like a trail, doesn't it? We could search in that area."

Dillon did another shrug of shoulders that still needed to fill out. "Maybe, but you're still talking a lot of area to search, boss. Acres and acres. It would take a lot of people to find anything in that wilderness."

Jackson laughed and leaned back in his chair. "I'm not talking people, Dillon."

Rhea narrowed her gaze and searched Jackson's features for some sign of what he was thinking, but failed. "What are you talking about, Jax?"

Chapter Eighteen

"LIDAR."

"LIDAR? What's that?" Dillon asked.

Jackson clapped the young man on the back. "I thought you young guys were all about the tech," he teased and then explained, "It's like RADAR, but using laser light to make 3D images of an area."

"3D images of lots and lots of trees," Rhea said dejectedly.

"Actually not," Jackson said. "I've been reading about how you combine LIDAR images with software that can actually strip away vegetation to reveal any hidden structures."

Dillon mimicked opening the pages of a book. "Reading, like on paper."

"On paper and on the net. My cousins have been trying to keep me from becoming a Luddite," Jackson quipped.

"Can your cousins help us with the software part of it?" Rhea asked, losing a little bit of the glumness that had filled her tone a moment ago.

"I'm sure Robbie and Sophie can help us with the software. Maybe they even know someone in the area with drones equipped with LIDAR. Depending on what the images show, Dillon here can help us hike into the area. Maybe the forest service, as well. It is in their jurisdiction after all," Jackson advised.

Jackson's desk phone rang and he hit the button to engage the speaker. "What's up, Rodriguez?"

"I have a visitor for you. He says Marcus sent him over," Millie said.

"Perfect. Please put him in the conference room. We'll be over in a second," he said and disengaged the speaker.

"That's good news, right?" Rhea said, suddenly feeling more optimistic than she had barely minutes before.

Jackson nodded. "For sure." He turned to Dillon and shook his hand. "Thanks for the help. We'll let you know when we need you again."

Dillon did a little salute. "Anytime, boss."

He exited, and Jackson gestured for Rhea to follow him. Once in the hallway, he laid a hand at her back in a way that was becoming achingly familiar. It offered immediate comfort and a sense of protection.

He guided her toward the conference room where an older man sat, waiting for them. He looked familiar, and as she dug through her memory, she recalled that she'd seen him tending the bar at the pub.

He stood as they entered, and Jackson held his hand out for a shake. She guessed that his use of the conference room and friendliness were intended to put the man at ease and not make him feel as if he was being interrogated. "Bradley, right?" Jackson said.

The man dipped his head in greeting in her direction and said, "That's right. You have a good memory, Detective."

"Jackson, please. Thanks for coming by," Jackson said and sat kitty-corner to the man. Rhea sat beside Jackson, opposite the bartender.

"New manager says to come by, I come by. I don't want no trouble," the man said, hands clasped before him on the tabletop. His fingers were gnarly, arthritic. He also had assorted scars on his hands, nicks, cuts and even a larger silvery shape, like from a burn. Clearly the hands of a man who worked hard for his living. But also obviously a nervous man as he bounced those clasped hands on the surface of the table.

"I guess you know something about the two men we're interested in?" Jackson asked.

A slight lift of his shoulders was followed by, "Some, but not much. They come now and again. Usually when we're not as busy."

Which confirmed what Marcus had told them earlier, Rhea thought.

"Anything else?" Jackson pressed.

"They're rough. Not people persons. Mostly keep to themselves except...they've harassed some of the women," Bradley said.

"Marcus said they were booted from the place for that," Jackson said, trying to elicit more with the open question.

"They were. Not recently. After that they seemed to clean up their act, but they still creeped us out. The one brother seemed to be the leader and was just plain mean."

"Mean in what way?" Jackson said, obviously wondering as she was what had prompted that impression.

Bradley bounced his hands on the tabletop faster and, as if realizing what he was doing, suddenly pulled them down beneath the edge of the table. "He almost growls his orders. Never a smile. Never a tip, but I got the feeling they didn't have much money. Their clothes were raggedy and sometimes they smelled. Bad. If the girls didn't put out the pretzels and nuts in front of them fast enough, we'd hear it."

Jackson cupped his jaw and rubbed it thoughtfully. "Marcus said you all called them the 'Mountain Men.' Do you think they live up there?"

Bradley laughed and wobbled his head of salt-and-pepper hair back and forth. "It wouldn't surprise me if they hole up in a cave somewhere and, like bears, only come out of hibernation a couple of times a year."

Jackson continued with his questioning. "Anything else? Any names?"

The man shook his head, but then snapped his fingers. "I think the mean one called his brother 'Wade.' The older one was always warning his brother to stop one thing or another."

As if to confirm, Jackson said, "You think they're brothers?"

Bradley nodded vigorously. "I have an older brother, so I know how it goes. Totally brothers. And they look alike, I think. Hard to tell with all that hair."

Jackson peered in her direction for the briefest moment before returning his attention to the bartender. He rose and held his hand out to the other man. "Thank you so much for coming by, Bradley. You've been really, really helpful. If by any chance you remember anything else or see these guys—"

"You'll be the first person I call, Jackson," the man said as he shook Jackson's hand and once again dipped his head in Rhea's direction. "Miss. I hope you find out what happened with your sister."

With that, the older man exited the room.

"What do we do now?" she asked, wondering, but Jackson clearly had no doubt about their next steps.

"We call Avalon PD and suspend what they're doing about Davis. Then I'll check with our Search and Rescue guys to see if they have LIDAR and if not, time to talk to the cousins again."

"I HOPE THOSE images we got for you were helpful," Robbie said.

"They were, cuz, but the thing is…they've taken us in a new direction in the investigation," Jackson admitted and did a quick look at Rhea to gauge how she was handling that new direction.

"Wow, okay. I guess you need more help. Let me get Sophie on the line," Robbie said.

"Afternoon, Jackson," Sophie said as she came across the speaker.

"Our investigations are pointing to two suspects who may be squatting on federal lands. But it's a problem to do a traditional search on foot. Too large an area and too much underbrush and vegetation," Jackson explained.

Robbie let out a low whistle. "Tough luck, but there are ways to search using drones."

"And LIDAR," Sophie added.

Jackson smiled, and Rhea jumped in with, "Jackson thought we might be able to do it that way."

"You definitely can. First, you survey the area with drones equipped with LIDAR, and then you process that imagery to see what's beneath trees and other foliage," Sophie confirmed.

Jackson shared a look with Rhea. "We're hoping you can connect us to someone who can do the drone work."

The murmur of low voices drifted across the line. "We can do that, *primo*," Robbie said.

"And we have software to process that imagery for you," Sophie quickly added.

"Thank you so much! That would be fantastic," Rhea said, her tone excited and grateful.

"We need to call a couple of drone specialists to see who's free, but hopefully we can get back to you by later tonight," Robbie said.

"Appreciated, cuz. Your help has been invaluable. I don't know how we can repay you," Jackson said and prepared for what he was sure would come next.

"Bring your lady friend to Miami!" Sophie said enthusiastically.

Rhea glanced in his direction, and the heat in her look could have ignited a forest fire. It was easy to picture the two of them, holding hands and walking along Ocean Drive in South Beach.

Voice husky with desire, he said, "I'll definitely think about that. Thanks again, and we'll talk to you later."

He ended the call and peered at Rhea, hoping he hadn't misread her earlier signals. "I'm sorry my cousins involved you in the Miami thing."

Her gaze narrowed and grew a little more somber. "I guess you don't like that idea?"

He raised his hands to stop her from going somewhere negative. "I do like it. I'm just not sure where we're headed. I mean, we've kind of been forced together."

"Forced? Is that what happened last night?" she said, her tone getting harsher by the second.

"Hell, no, Rhea. Last night and this morning were amazing. But you're vulnerable right now, and I've got to think about—"

"Becoming police chief?" she said with an arch of her brow, the blue of her eyes becoming as chill as the ice on a winter lake.

"The investigation. And you. I never expected what's happening between us, but I don't regret it."

"I don't, either, Jax. But maybe we need to take a step back until this is all over," Rhea said.

He hated that she was right, but it made sense to bring things back into perspective until the investigation was done. And if his cousins could basically work a miracle and find something on the mountain that would lead them to their two new suspects, the investigation would quickly be coming to a close.

"I just want to update the digital notebook and reach out to my local contact at the Park Service and see how she wants us to handle this. I can have someone drive you home if you want," Jackson said.

Rhea shook her head. "I'll just hang out here and do some sketching."

She didn't give Jackson time to argue with her, since she grabbed her ever-present knapsack and pulled out her sketch pad and pencils. Balancing the pad on her knee, she went to work and he did, as well, adding all the information they'd gathered to his notes.

Rhea flipped to the sketch of Jackson that she had started just two days ago. It had the barebones lines of him lying on the sofa, but needed so much more to do justice to the man sitting across from her. Especially since she now had intimate knowledge of that body. The hard muscles sheathed in smooth skin. The scars of a warrior along his shoulder and back, making her wonder if that accounted for the pain she'd seen on occasion.

And his face. Lord, it was the face of a fallen angel, tempting a woman with his full lips, dimples and the slight cleft in his chin. Those features were balanced by the strong line of his jaw and sharp straight nose.

She worked on those elements, since she had an unfettered look at them as he worked, a slight furrow in his brow as he concentrated and pecked information into the computer. At one point he leaned back, rubbed his jaw with his hand, as if puzzled, but then he was back at work.

Smiling, she shifted her pencil lower, adding definition to the broad expanse of his chest and lean midsection. Capturing with her pencil and paper the details her hands had explored last night and this morning. Understanding, but regretting, that she wouldn't explore more of him tonight.

Caught up in her sketching, she was jolted back by the loud ring of Jackson's cell phone. He answered and said, "Hi, cuz. That's good news. Thanks."

With a swipe, she ended the call. "They've reached out to their contact and copied me on the email. Hopefully we'll be able to arrange to have the drone survey tomorrow."

"That's good news," she said, grateful and expectant, but also worried. As long as the investigation wasn't done, she'd be with Jackson and Selene was still alive. The next few days could change all that, but would it be for the better?

"Ready to go home?" he said, lacing his hands behind his head to stretch. A slight grimace skipped across his features, but he controlled it and brought his hands down to the arms of his chair to push to his feet.

"Back hurting?"

It was obvious he didn't want to appear vulnerable as he shrugged and said, "Just a kink. Too much sitting. They say sitting—"

"Is the new smoking," she finished for him with a chuckle. "We're both in professions where we do a lot of sitting."

"Too late for a hike, but maybe we can think of something else to do." His gaze met hers, the gray of it smoky, warning of the fire that might soon ignite.

"For sure," she said, despite her earlier reservations, and held her hand out to him in invitation.

As he slipped his work-rough hand in hers, she told herself not to worry about tonight or tomorrow. Whatever was meant to be was meant to be.

Even if it brought heartache.

THE TENSION HAD been building ever since they'd left the police station and grabbed a quick bite for dinner in one of the restaurants along Main Street. Night had fallen as Jackson let them into his home, the ever-present police cruiser sitting in the driveway to warn off whoever had burned down Jackson's shed.

Inside, they paused at the base of the stairs, the tension so thick it felt like a presence shimmering between them.

With a wave of his hand, Jackson pushed away that sensation and said, "I have some things to do in my office. Why don't you go up and get settled?"

Coward! Rhea wanted to scream, hating that he'd put the onus on her to decide where she'd spend the night because, well, she was feeling as craven as he was. With a curt nod, she stomped up the stairs, annoyed. Anxious. Needy. Despite knowing what was happening between them was so uncertain, she still wanted him. She wanted to not waste a minute with him because once the investigation was over...

She wouldn't think about that.

She wouldn't think about what she would do if Selene...

No, I won't think that. She's out there. Somewhere, she told herself and walked to the guest bedroom to get her nightshirt. A nice hot shower was bound to relax her and buy some time until Jackson came up and then...

She hurried into the shower, but took her time luxuriating beneath the rain showerhead, working shampoo into a thick lather. Soaping up and running her hands across her skin. Letting the heat of the water sink into her bones. Thick steam gathered in the room, warning her she'd been in there for quite some time.

Reluctantly she shut off the water, grabbed a towel and dried off. Her skin seemed sensitized as the touch of the terry cloth across her body roused memories of the feel of the sheets beneath her, and Jackson above her, his big body driving into her.

The warmth on her skin from the water morphed into a different kind of heat deep within.

Rushing into Jackson's bedroom, she didn't even waste a moment to turn on the light. She slipped beneath the sheets and pulled them tight about her, the bed feeling empty without him. Her senses hyper, tuned to the slightest noise until she heard the first footfall on the steps.

She held her breath, waiting for him. Eager for his body next to hers.

The footfalls came closer and paused at the door. A breath seemed to burst from him, almost as if he'd been holding it in anticipation. A rush of steps came before his weight settled on the edge of the bed.

"Rhea," he said softly. Hesitantly.

She glanced at him. His face was in partial shadow, the only light that from the hallway. It made it hard to gauge what he was thinking. But then he cradled her jaw and tenderly ran his thumb across her cheek. Drifted it down to her lips, where he traced the edges of it, as powerful as any kiss. Stirring awake desire.

"Touch me, Jax," she said and covered his hand with hers. Urged it to her breast where her nipple pebbled beneath his rough palm.

"Rhea, this is crazy," he said, but he strummed his thumb across the hard tip and then reached beneath the sheets to find the hem of her night-shirt and draw it off her body.

With eager fingers she undid the buttons on his uniform shirt, baring his chest to her. Sitting up to drop kisses across the expanse until she tongued his masculine nipple and he groaned and held her head to him. With a little love bite, she brought her hands to his sides and urged him down to her, wanting his skin against hers. Wanting his hands on her.

"Please, Jax. Please," she pleaded.

Jackson moved away from her only long enough to remove the rest of his clothes and slip beneath the sheets with her.

She had her hands on him instantly, cupping him and stroking his hard length.

"I want you in me," she said and pressed him close.

"Bossy, aren't you?" he teased, drawing a chuckle from her as he fumbled in the nightstand for a condom. He had barely taken it out, and she was shifting, urging him to his back and taking it from him. She tore it open, took out the condom and, with delicious leisure, rolled it down over him, and now it was his turn to plead.

"Rhea. I need you," he said, and she didn't disappoint.

She straddled him and sank onto him, slowly.

He laid his hands on her hips. Guided her to move on him, riding him. Thrusting into her forcefully, driving until the release washed over them, stealing their breaths.

Rhea wrapped her arms around him and laid her head against his chest. His heart beat rapidly beneath her ear, and his skin was damp. He smelled of man, leather and Jackson. She inhaled that aroma to commit it to memory. To remember it long past when this moment was done. He made her feel loved, but she told herself not to think too much about that.

There was still too much to do. Too many unknowns.

And when the morning came, it might be the beginning of the end depending on what the drone footage revealed. Much like the end of the investigation would reveal if whatever she was feeling for Jackson was real.

Chapter Nineteen

The drone sitting on the ground before them in the bright morning light was nothing like the small drones Rhea had seen at various events in Denver. The drone was easily a good three feet or more across, with large propellers to lift it high into the air. It sat on two upraised legs and nestled at the center was something that looked like a camera, but she guessed was the LIDAR device, whatever that was. Projecting above the body of the drone, almost on antennae, were some pod-like pieces.

Jackson and the drone operator had gathered by the police cruiser, where Jackson had spread out the map of the mountain area above. He instructed the other man on what they wanted to survey. As she approached, she heard the drone operator issue a low whistle, look up toward the mountains and rub his head.

"Lots of dense vegetation, but hopefully the laser will be able to get through to get the data we need for Robbie and Sophie," the man said.

"What if there isn't enough data, Rick?" Jackson asked, taking the words right out of her mouth.

With a shrug, Rick said, "Robbie and Sophie are miracle workers. They can probably download topographical maps of the area and work them into any analysis to fill in gaps."

"Will it take long?" Rhea asked.

Rick peered up at the mountains again and said, "Your cousins sent me the specs for several flight plans. I've programmed them into my tablet, and once we send up the drone, it will fly those plans on its own to collect the data. My guess is a couple of hours."

"And then you send the data to my cousins?" Jackson said.

Rick nodded. "I'll transmit it to them, and they'll use their programs to get whatever images you want." Knowing what question would come next, Rick added, "With their supercomputers, it shouldn't take too long to process the data. You'd probably have it tomorrow if they jump right on it."

"Sounds good, and thanks again for doing this," Jackson said.

"Anything I can do. I can only imagine how hard it must be for you, Rhea. Hopefully we'll be able to help you find your sister," Rick said and walked to his tablet and remote controls. He picked up the controls, and a second later, the propellers whirred to life. With some swipes on the tablet, the drone lifted off and sped toward the mountains.

Jackson and she leaned against the cruiser and watched the drone disappear up the mountain, but the hum of the propellers gave testament that it was still there, working its way along the first of the flight plans that Jackson's cousins had programmed. Rick walked back toward them, his gaze locked on his tablet. As he neared, he held it up for them to see the images that the drone was capturing.

"Lots and lots of trees," Rhea said, slightly worried that was all the imagery would capture.

Rick nodded, but seeing her concerns, he explained. "That's what our eyes and the camera see, but the LIDAR is getting a lot more. Trust me."

"We do," Jackson said and laid his arm over her shoulder to draw her near with a reassuring squeeze.

"We trust you, Rick," she added, almost in apology for having any doubts.

"Great. Let me get back to watching, just in case," he said and walked away to keep an eye on the drone's footage, the remote control nearby. She assumed that was just in case there was a problem with any of the flight plans.

The chill of morning faded as an hour passed, and then another, as the drone flew flight plan after flight plan. Jackson and she sat on a blanket spread beneath the shade of a large aspen, sipping coffee from the large thermos they'd brought with them. Taking over some coffee and breakfast pastries to Rick while he monitored the drone.

It was almost lunch hour when the drone came whirring back and landed just yards away from them. They approached as the blades stopped whirring, and Rick walked over to the machine. He worked quickly to remove the LIDAR device and store it in its protective luggage.

Jackson helped him with packing up the rest of the equipment, and once they were done, Jackson said, "What do you do next?"

Rick gestured to the luggage with the LIDAR device. "I'm going to connect that to my computer and get the data uploaded to the cloud. Once that's done, I'll let Robbie and Sophie know so they can generate the information for you."

Jackson nodded and shook the man's hand. "Thanks again. If there's ever anything we can do for you—"

"I'll let you know. Maybe help me score some BBQ from Declan's place. I hear it's the best in the area," Rick said.

Jackson smiled. "It is. Whenever you want to head over there, I'll let him know you're coming and it's on me. Whatever you want."

"Thanks, Jax. And good luck with everything. Rhea," the man said with a deferential nod.

Jackson and Rhea helped Rick load all the equipment containers in the back of his van. After another handshake from Jackson and hug from her, Rick drove off.

Rhea hoped that they'd gotten what they needed. With Matt virtually eliminated as a suspect, they had to focus on whether the two men at the pub had possibly had a part in Selene's disappearance, the attacks against her and the destruction at Jackson's home.

Jackson laid a hand on her shoulder and drew her near, comforting her. "This will work," he said with a playful nudge, trying to lighten the mood.

"It will," she said with more confidence than she was feeling and with anticipation. His cousins' supercomputers couldn't work fast enough as far as she was concerned, but she knew everyone involved would work as quickly as possible.

But in the meantime, they had little to do and she was too antsy to just sit around. She was even too antsy to sketch, which rarely happened. Jackson must have sensed her mood, since he said, "It's a beautiful day. Feel like a walk around town?"

She'd love a walk, but didn't want to deal with having other people around. She wanted something more private where it just the two of them. "Anywhere it can be just the two of us?"

Jackson peered at her and nodded. "I know just the place. How about we pick up a picnic lunch?"

She smiled. "That sounds nice. Thank you."

In just over fifteen minutes, they had a picnic lunch from one of the restaurants in Regina and were back on the road. Not far past the lake and nearby spillway, Jackson turned off onto a side road that ran parallel to the lake. Every now and then he'd look back, as if to check if anyone was following, but apparently satisfied they were alone, he continued on their trek. To the right of the paved road was what looked like a hiking trail that ran for some distance.

Less than a quarter mile from the turnoff, they pulled up in front of a large cabin that faced the lake. It reminded her of Jackson's home, and when they pulled into the driveway, she noticed the mailbox with the owner's name: Whitaker.

"Is this your family's place?" she asked as Jackson parked the cruiser.

"Mom and Dad's place. While they're in Florida, I come up here every week or so to make sure everything is in order. It's got nice views of the lake. I figured we could have lunch up on the front porch and then do a short hike along the trail. If you want, that is."

"I'd like that," she said. She also liked that he asked and didn't assume, unlike her last boyfriend. An artist like her, it had started off well at first, but then he'd become more and more demanding. More controlling until she had finally put an end to the relationship. In the couple of years since then, she'd stayed out of the dating game, focusing on her artwork and building her business.

She wasn't sure she could call what was happening with her and Jackson dating, or call him her boyfriend. It was way more than that.

He grabbed the bag with their food from the back seat and swung around to open her door, ever the gentleman. The comforting touch of his hand came at her back, the pressure gentle as he guided her up the long set of steps up to the generous front porch for the cabin.

The porch wrapped around the cabin. In the front there were two large rockers and between them a small circular table where he set the bag with their lunch. As Rhea swept past him to one of the rockers, Jackson removed their sandwiches, chips and soda from the bag and laid it all out on the table.

They settled on the rockers to sit and eat, their words few as they satisfied their hunger, but maybe also possibly because they were both thinking about what had happened that morning and where it might lead.

For Rhea, there was no doubt the end was near. If the images found nothing, the investigation would go cold again. If there *was* something on the images…it would help them find her sister, and she refused to give up hope that Selene was alive.

Jackson took a last bite of his sandwich, scooped up a handful of chips and popped a few into his mouth. He chewed thoughtfully, swallowed and said, "I think it went well this morning."

"I think so, although I'm not really into tech. Not a Luddite, mind you, but I like doing things hands-on."

He raised an eyebrow and fixed his gaze on her. It was hot, so hot. "I like that you like that."

Rhea's cheeks burned with the heat ignited by his look. She shook her head and chuckled. "I'll have to remember that."

"And me? Will you remember me?" Jackson said, his mood growing more somber.

Remember him? How can I ever forget him? She reached over and laid her hand on his forearm. With a tender stroke, she said, "I could never forget you, Jax. What we have…it's complicated, isn't it?"

"It is, but you're very special to me, Rhea. Whatever happens…" He wagged his head in an almost defeated gesture, laced his fingers with hers and offered her a sad smile. "How about that hike?"

"Sounds nice," she said, eager to move away from a discussion that could only bring sadness.

Hand-in-hand they walked down the steps and across the one-lane road to a small path that led to the trail by the lake. Sunlight frolicked on the surface of the lake, glittering like silver and ice-blue confetti against the cerulean blue waters. Waters that lapped softly along the reeds at the lake's edges.

Ducks and geese swam here and there on the surfaces, dark shapes against the light dancing on the lake. Far ahead of them, wading in the grasses on long sticklike legs, a great blue heron stood still, patient. Waiting to snare a meal. They carefully walked past so as not to disturb the bird and pushed on, voices silent. Thoughts loud, but calming slowly thanks to the beauty of the nature around them. A little farther up the trail, the sudden and loud flap of wings alerted them to a large bird taking flight.

A bald eagle soared into view over the lake, majestic and immense. With a few flaps of its wings the eagle climbed ever higher, then glided on a burst of breeze, reveling in its freedom.

JACKSON WATCHED THE regal bird soar and dance on the wind. Its flight graceful, but filled with strength. In some ways, Rhea was like that bird. Elegant. Powerful. Free.

He had to remind himself of that. Free to choose her own path. Free to leave when the time came, but much like the bald eagles who left in late winter, sometimes a pair would stay behind to nest and build a family.

They walked together for a good hour, enjoying the many sights along the lake. The spring weather was perfect for their walk, with a slight breeze to combat the heat building from the bright sunlight. In the shade of the trees on the trail, it was almost a little chilly and when Rhea shivered, he wrapped an arm around her shoulders and drew her close.

Hips bumping, they finally turned around and strolled back toward his parents' home, peace filling him. Funny, really, if you thought about it. He was in the middle of an active investigation. Someone was trying to hurt her, maybe even kill her, and yet what he felt was a peace that he hadn't experienced in years.

His heart was huge with that peace, with love for her, as they got back into the cruiser to head back to the police station for another look through their notes and to see if anyone needed his help on any other cases. The chief had warned him about how the investigation was taking too much of his time and the town's resources. With some downtime until his cousins came through with the information from the LIDAR footage, he had to give his attention to other cases his colleagues might be working on.

Back at the police station, he did just that, leaving Rhea comfortably tucked away in his office sketching while he checked in with the other officers on the force. He assisted one with recreating the scene of a hit-and-run. At another desk, an officer asked for advice about a burglary and that officer's version of the entry into the building.

Pleased with being of help to his colleagues, he was returning to his office when his police chief walked back into the station. If he remembered correctly, his boss had had a meeting with the mayor and some members of the town council about the police budget for the coming year.

"How'd it go, Bill?" he asked, hoping for positive news.

The police chief lifted his meaty shoulders in a careless way. "It's too soon to know, but at least it wasn't an immediate rejection."

Jackson heard the tone of worry in his chief's voice. "Which might happen if they get a whiff of any issues. Like Selene's case, right?"

His boss glared at him. "Like that, Jax. I told you that when you first decided on this lunacy. Have you made any progress?"

Jackson clenched his jaw, biting back his anger. With a cleansing breath, he said, "We have. We've pretty much eliminated Matt Davis as a suspect. I've called Avalon PD to let them know that. We have photos of two possible suspects and a witness who saw their vehicle by the victim's sedan the night of her disappearance. Once we have the results of some drone imagery, we may know their whereabouts."

Taken aback, possibly shamed, the chief blustered, "Well, that all sounds good, Jax. Keep me posted."

The older man hurried away and Jackson returned to his office, where Rhea was still bent over her sketch pad, drawing.

"It's almost six. Are you ready to go? Maybe get dinner?" he said, but as he walked toward her his smartphone chirped. He grabbed it off his desk and realized it was his cousin Robbie calling.

"Hey, Robbie. Do you have good news for us?"

Rhea's head popped up at the sound of his cousin's name.

"Putting you on speaker," he said as he walked over to Rhea and sat in the chair beside her, the smartphone held between them.

"Okay. I've got Sophie here with me, and like I said, good news. We were able to process the LIDAR data and get some images for you. How about a video call and a bigger screen, so we can explain the information?"

"I'll arrange that. I'd also like to include one of my colleagues who is familiar with the area," he said.

"Great. I'll send a link to the meeting. Fifteen minutes?" Sophie asked.

"We'll be ready," Jackson said and hung up. He shared a look with Rhea and hoped she would be.

Chapter Twenty

Jackson had set up a large projection monitor in the conference room and sat next to her, a laptop before him ready to make the video call. Officer Dillon sat across from them at the table, poised with pen and paper to take notes if necessary.

Following the link Sophie had sent, Jackson began the video call. The almost musical beep-bloop-beep chime ended quickly as Robbie and Sophie answered and their smiling faces jumped onto the big screen in front of them.

Even if she hadn't been told that they were Jackson's cousins, she would have seen the family resemblance. They both had the same square jaw, straight nose and thumbprint cleft in their chins. Broad dimples bracketed their mouths, and like Jackson, they had light eyes, although it was hard to tell what color thanks to the quality of the video combined with the projection.

Jackson's hair was a light brown, but Robbie and Sophie both had coffee brown, slightly wavier locks. Robbie was handsome. Sophie beautiful, but not in a classic way. More like a warrior goddess, strong and sure of herself.

"Happy to see you, *primo*," she said.

"Happy to see the both of you, and thank you again. I've got Rhea and Officer Dillon with me," he said, although he was the only one visible on the video call thanks to the angle of the laptop's camera.

"Like I said before, we've got good news for you," Robbie said and, a second later, a photo replaced their smiling images.

"We took the LIDAR images, and this is the raw photo," Robbie said, describing the first image. "There's lots of forest on both mountains, except for the ski resort to the extreme right and an obvious trail near that area."

As Robbie spoke, the mouse highlighted the areas his cousin was describing. When he shifted to the path close to the resort, Dillon spoke up. "That's the trail that most hikers use."

After that, Robbie continued, pointing toward the middle of the photo. "Here there appears to be slightly less vegetation, but then it's quite dense to the left of it."

Dillon rose from his spot and walked toward the screen. Gesturing to the area where the forest was less dense, he said, "I think this is the old logging road I told you about. I'm not sure just how passable the road is nowadays, and I don't think many people use it."

"Thanks for that info, Officer Dillon," Sophie said. "There was clearly something there even before we processed the image with our software."

When she finished, another image immediately popped up on the screen, surprising them with the look of it. All vegetation had been cleared away, revealing the contours of the mountainside, as well as what appeared to be other features.

Robbie came back online and continued with his explanation. "We downloaded a topographical map so we could have reference points to assist us in determining what was natural and what was man-made. Beside the resort area that was visible before, the processed image reveals several buildings beneath the tree line close to the resort and the path of the nearby trail."

"Wow, way cool," Officer Dillon said.

Very, Rhea thought as Sophie took over, explaining the other features revealed by their work. "There is clearly a break of some kind on the second mountain. I think Officer Dillon mentioned it was an old logging trail. But fairly high up on the trail, there's a small structure. Maybe a lean-to of some kind."

"Would that be big enough to hide a vehicle?" Jackson asked.

"For sure," Sophie answered and pressed onward. "About two miles away there's another structure. A cabin. See this square at one side? Probably a chimney."

"You're sure that's a cabin?" Jackson asked.

"Without a doubt," Robbie said and then shifted to an image zoomed and enhanced to show the details of the structure. After that, he displayed several other photos, from slightly different angles, which helped to define the path of the logging trail, as well as a possible trail from the lean-to toward the cabin.

When he finished, he said, "We've sent you these photos via email. If you need us to testify to them, we'd be happy to do that."

"We totally appreciate all you've done," Rhea said, suddenly feeling very optimistic about what the photos had revealed.

"We never say 'No' to family," Sophie said, which prompted a rough laugh from Jackson.

"Hint duly noted, as well as massive guilt, Sophie. I love you guys, and I hope to see you soon," Jackson said.

"Hope to see you soon *in Miami, primo*," Robbie said and ended the video call.

"They sure know how to lay on the guilt," Rhea teased, and Jackson laughed. He shot to his feet to turn on the lights in the conference room, leaned against the wall and crossed his arms. Peering at Dillon, he said, "You mentioned that logging road might be tough to traverse."

Dillon nodded. "Might be. We'd obviously need 4x4s and additional manpower. Those guys are probably armed."

Jackson nodded. "I spoke to the Parks Service, and they're leaving it up to us to take action. I'm thinking two other officers, SWAT possibly, if the chief approves of course."

"I agree. Weather tomorrow is supposed to be good," Dillon said.

Almost too eagerly, Rhea thought.

"I'll speak to the chief and ask him who will be our backup, but remember this, Dillon. These men are likely dangerous. Possibly murderers, or kidnappers if Selene is still alive," Jackson said in warning, likewise sensing the young officer's almost misplaced enthusiasm.

"Alive? It's been over six months, boss. Sorry, miss," Dillon said with a guilty look in her direction.

"It's okay, Officer Dillon. I understand." She peered at Jackson as he continued to lean against the wall.

As her gaze met his, determination filled his gaze, but also pain. They were possibly almost at the end of their journey. It might end at a most dangerous place tomorrow, after they made their ascent up the mountain and to the structures the images had revealed.

"I'm going with you tomorrow, Jax. Make no mistake about that," she warned.

"We'll discuss this later. Right now, I have to get the chief's approval for this operation."

He didn't wait for a reply from either her or Dillon. He rushed out, his face dark with worry and hurt, gray eyes as stormy as rainclouds. His lips a thin line in a face as stony as granite. Closed off from her, and she understood. He wasn't just preparing himself for the danger to come.

He was preparing for her to leave.

HE MOVED IN HER, his big body driving her toward release. His gaze locked on her, wanting to see when she went over and to hold that moment close before he lost control.

Her blue eyes had darkened, were almost black with desire. A soft moan escaped her with one thrust, and he worried he might have hurt her until she dug her fingernails into his skin and arched her back, deepening his penetration. He thrust again and she urged him on, wrapping her legs around him.

Inside pressure built, his heart pounding harder and louder. Almost as if calling out what he was feeling. *Love you, love you, love you*, but the words never left his mouth, trapped by fear.

Beneath him, her body shuddered and tightened, and she called out his name, her release washing over her. Spilling onto him as he drove into her one last time. Her name escaped his lips and he fell over with her.

He held his weight off her, but then she reached up and cradled his shoulders. Invited him to rest on her, their bodies still united. But after a short minute, he rolled onto his side and took her with him, tucking her close.

They lay there in silence until Rhea stroked a hand across his chest. "It's going to be okay."

A rough laugh escaped him. "Funny. I thought that was supposed to be my line."

She didn't respond, she just moved closer, her hand resting over his heart.

He understood. As much as he had searched for the words since they'd left the police station earlier, he hadn't found them. Hadn't been able to figure out how to tell her that he loved her. How that had happened in just a few days. What he hoped for the future with her. If there even was a future.

Rhea rested beside him, her hand tucked over his heart, listening to the beat as it settled into a steady rhythm. She felt his tension growing. The muscles beneath her hand were tight, unyielding. The arm resting down her back, keeping her near, didn't exude that feeling of comfort or protection that his touch usually did.

It made her wonder if it would be okay, as she'd said earlier. If after tomorrow, no matter what happened, they could make this relationship work. If they could explore the love that had somehow blossomed between them at such an unlikely time. But it had taken hold and sunk its roots deep in her heart.

Has it done the same in him?

She refused to think that it hadn't, but tomorrow would tell. No matter what happened, they might have to go their separate ways.

But can we find our way back together?

Chapter Twenty-One

The turnoff to the logging road was blocked by a wall of underbrush, but the tire tracks in the soft dirt confirmed it had been recently used. Jackson and Dillon got out of the SUV and, after examining the tumble of vines and brush, pulled it away to allow them to pass.

They bumped their way up the uneven road, which was fairly navigable despite the large boulders and soft loose dirt at numerous spots along the path. At one point, the SUV behind them carrying the two members of the Regina SWAT team got bogged down in one of the softer ruts. Jackson got out, cut down some branches with his machete and tucked them under the tires, providing the traction to get them out of the rut.

Inside their SUV, Dillon manned a tablet with software that Robbie and Sophie had provided, which visualized exactly where they were based on the LIDAR images. As Dillon lifted the tablet, a 3D rendering of the area around them sprang to life. But as they got closer to the first structure identified by the drone imagery, they didn't need a tablet to tell them what was right before their eyes: the SUV from the photos at the pub.

Jackson got out of the car, stood on the running board and gestured to everyone to hold their positions with his upraised fist.

He hopped off the running board and carefully approached the lean-to, which housed the SUV, worried that anyone who had taken the time to hide the turnoff for the road might have created a booby trap to protect the vehicle.

He inched his way all around the area, searching for trip wires or hidden traps.

"All clear," he said and gave the hand motion to go.

Everyone exited the vehicles and came over to examine the SUV against the pub photo.

"Definitely the same car," said the one SWAT officer as he stood in front of the Jeep, his rifle slung across his chest.

Jackson squatted to examine the custom bumper. There were rough gouges and scratches in the thick steel, a testament to when they'd used the vehicle to ram them. There were even still some hints of white paint from the police cruiser's bumper.

"This is the vehicle that attacked us." He straightened and faced his team.

"These men are dangerous. They are likely armed. We need to use extreme caution on our approach and you—" he gestured to Rhea "—you hang back and stay close."

Jackson hated that she was even with them, but Rhea had insisted, and he knew it wouldn't have done any good to argue with her. They had come so far together, and it would end with them together. He walked over to her, cupped her jaw and said, "You understand, right? I don't want to see you hurt." For good measure, he checked the bulletproof vest and helmet she wore, making sure she'd be secure.

Rhea cradled his face. "I understand. I'll stay close, because I don't want to see any of you hurt."

He nodded and went to the head of his team. Gave the Move-out symbol.

There was a narrow trail from the SUV lean-to westward, and they hiked on it cautiously, watching for booby traps or alarms. Checking the tablet to see just how close they were to the cabin, which had been revealed by the LIDAR.

Jackson figured the structure was a good two miles from the logging trail. Not a long hike normally, but he and the other officers were in full protective gear. It was hot and sweaty beneath the body armor and helmets. Still they pressed on, navigating the trail until the cabin came into view, just where the LIDAR had said it would be.

He gave the Hold command and examined the clearing around the structure. Off to one side, there was an area with a woodpile and log with an ax buried in it.

One less weapon for them, Jackson thought.

Crude chairs fashioned from branches graced an equally crude and rustic porch, clearly an add-on to an otherwise solid log cabin. Curtains in an indiscriminate color hung on the windows, blocking his view into the building.

Wood smoke escaped the chimney, and the smell of it drifted over to them along with the scent of bacon. Someone was making a meal. Maybe a late breakfast.

A good thing. It meant they were home and maybe not paying too much attention to the exterior of the cabin.

He gestured to his team members to come close, and once they had gathered around him, he spoke to them in a low tone, directing each member to a different side of the structure. With a quick glance at Rhea, he said, "You stay down and close to me. Understand?"

Rhea nodded, comprehending Jackson's concerns. But there was no way she was going to miss this moment after all that they'd been through to get here.

She hung back, as close as she could so as not to hamper Jackson, and watched as the other team members fanned out. They had only gotten about halfway to their positions when a clanging sound rang out. A cow bell, warning anyone in the cabin that someone was outside.

The SWAT member who had tripped the alarm dropped to the ground, trying to avoid detection, but a second later came the sound of glass breaking and a shot rang out in his direction. Bark flew off a tree in his general direction.

A curtain shifted in the front of the cabin, and the glass shattered as a second rifle barrel poked out.

Jackson muttered a curse and shook his head. With a backward sweep of his arm, he tucked Rhea behind the protection of his back. Having been discovered, he had no choice but to shout, "Police. Drop your weapons and come out with your hands up."

A round of gunshots came in their direction, smashing into the trees and brush around them. One of their team returned fire, but Jackson radioed them and said, "Hold your fire. They could have a hostage in there."

He again called out to the men in the cabin. "We don't have to do this the hard way. Surrender, and I can speak to the DA to keep the sentence reasonable."

In response, a female face suddenly appeared in the window, but then was hauled back abruptly. "We'll kill her," someone shouted.

Selene. Alive. Selene's alive, Rhea thought and

stood up slightly, her gut reaction to run to her sister.

Jackson hauled her back down and looked over his shoulder at her. Blood dripped from a cut on his cheekbone and a bit of bark stuck to his helmet. Eyes hard, he said, "Steady, Rhea."

Without missing a beat, he turned back toward the cabin and screamed, "You can make this easier for yourselves. Let the woman go, and I'll talk to the DA."

More gunfire erupted, but it was followed by shouting from inside the cabin. The thick log walls were enough to muffle whatever it was they were saying to each other, but Rhea hoped they were talking about surrendering. Her hopes were dashed as bullets tore into the underbrush and ground all around the SWAT officer who had tripped the cowbell.

A volley of gunfire erupted from the officer toward the side of the cabin. The dull thud of bullets striking wood reverberated through her.

Once again, Jackson reined in the response. "Hold your fire. Repeat, hold your fire."

"Copy that," echoed from all the officers.

The creak of the door drew their attention. It opened, almost in slow motion, providing a partial view of the interior of the cabin. But then suddenly, Selene stood in the doorway, hands held on top of her head.

She paused, a little wobbly. *Way too thin,*

Rhea thought. The tattered shirt hung on her slim shoulders and was stained in various spots. Rhea had given her the shirt two Christmases ago. Her jeans were worn and torn, likewise dirty as if from soot or soil.

"Come forward slowly, hands up," Jackson shouted.

Selene took another hesitant step toward them onto the front porch. She squinted, as if the sunlight was too much for her, making Rhea wondered if it had been months since she'd been outside the walls of her prison.

"Walk forward slowly," Jackson said as another burst of shouting came from within the cabin.

A bearded face became visible in the window, and the man called out, "You have her. Now leave us alone."

More fighting followed that declaration, and with the door open, the words were a little more discernable. One voice, stronger and obviously in command. "Shut the door. Shut the damn door."

The second, weaker, almost stumbling. "B-b-b-ut—"

"Shut it," boomed the first person, and the door slammed closed.

Selene jumped, almost as if shot, and it was all Rhea could do not to run to her sister. But Jackson had his arm stuck out, a barrier keeping her back.

The shouting resumed inside the cabin, and

Jackson took advantage of that to stand, exposing himself to gunfire. He held out his hand and motioned to Selene. "Here. Come here, Selene."

Her sister's eyes widened, but then she ran toward them and dropped to her knees, into Rhea's arms, when she got there.

Rhea kissed her sister's face and wrapped her arms around her, unable to believe she was really there. That she was alive.

"You've made this easier for yourselves, but you've got to surrender. Come out, hands up," Jackson commanded.

More yelling came from the cabin, followed by an assortment of crashes, as if someone was trashing the place. More shouts, and then silence. Finally, surprising all of them, the sound of a single gunshot.

Jackson sucked in a breath, trying to fathom what that single gunshot might mean. Especially as the door slowly opened again and a hesitant voice called out, "D-d-don't shoot. Please don't h-h-urt m-m-e."

There was almost a nervous quality to the voice, warning him that it might be the younger brother. A gentle hand on his forearm drew his attention back to where Rhea and Selene huddled, arms around each other. It was Selene's hand, and as he met her gaze, so much like Rhea's, he was taken aback for a moment. But only a millisecond in this life and death situation.

"It's Wade," Selene confirmed.

Jackson nodded. "Come out slowly, Wade. Hands on your head. We won't hurt you."

Finally, someone appeared in the doorway. One of the men in the photos. One of Selene's kidnappers.

"Slowly, Wade," he repeated as the man faltered on the front porch, clearly afraid as his gaze darted all around, seemingly uncomprehending.

Wade took a few more uncertain steps into the clearing in front of the cabin.

Over his shoulder, Jackson asked Selene, "What's his brother's name?"

"Earl," she said harshly, as if it pained her to say his name.

"On your knees, Wade. Where's Earl?" Jackson said, rising slightly so Wade could see him, but keeping behind the trunk of the tree for safety.

"Dead. Kilt himself," Wade said and whipped his head in the direction of the cabin.

Jackson radioed his team. "Visuals? Can anyone confirm?"

Dillon spoke up first. "I can see into the cabin. Looks like a body on the floor."

"Are you sure, Dillon?" Jackson pressed, wanting to avoid any additional bloodshed.

"I'm sure, boss."

Jackson commanded the two SWAT officers. "Levine. Anderson. Move in. Dillon, hang back and secure our suspect when possible."

"Copy that," all the officers confirmed.

Jackson waited, protecting the two women while his counterparts hurried toward the cabin, guns drawn. The SWAT officers paused at the door. Entry areas like that could be a fatal funnel, but as the one officer peered inside, he lowered his weapon slightly.

"Shot himself in the head. Going in to check on him. Cover my six, Anderson," Officer Levine said and entered the cabin. He emerged a second later and gave the All-clear motion.

Jackson stood and helped Rhea bring her sister to her feet. Together, they supported her to walk to a stump, where she sat and gazed up at them, tears streaming down her face.

"I thought I'd die here...like the others," she said, and her gaze skittered back to the cabin for a second and then back to them.

"Others?" Jackson asked, hands on his hips as he focused on Selene's face, so much like Rhea's, but so much thinner from her captivity. The remnants of a bruise, going yellowish and purple, lingered along her right cheek. He clenched his jaw with anger at the thought of anyone striking her.

Selene nodded. "Wade let it slip that they'd taken other women, but I already knew. There were other feminine things in the cabin. Combs. Jewelry. Clothes. I think they killed them."

"Anderson. Dillon. Levine. Secure the area. I'm going to call in the Crime Scene Unit, since we may have other victims here," Jackson instructed and then stepped away to phone his chief and advise him on their status and the possibility they had multiple kidnappings and homicides.

"I have to say I'm surprised, Jax. That's just not the kind of thing that happens here," the chief said.

"I'm with you, Bill. I'm hoping Selene is wrong, and it was just Wade shoplifting things, like he did in Regina, but if not…" If not they had serial killers on their hands.

"I'll get them up there ASAP. How's the woman? Do you need transport to take her to the hospital?"

Jackson glanced back toward where Selene sat, Rhea kneeling beside her. "She's shaky, Chief. We may need transport, but give me a little more time to talk with her and see what she wants."

Jackson returned to the two women and was once again struck by how identical they were. Same intelligent crystal-blue eyes and full lips. The dark, almost black hair, although Selene's was far longer and dull. As he neared, they both looked toward him, the motion of their bodies in unison.

"CSU will be coming up to search the scene and preserve evidence. I'd like to take you to the hospital—"

"No, I want to go home," Selene said, shaking her head furiously.

Jackson looked toward Rhea, who did a little dip of her head. "I think that would be best."

Blowing out a rough breath, Jackson said, "We need to take some photos of you and get a statement. Are you up for doing that?"

Selene nodded. "I am. Anything you need me to do."

"I'm grateful for that, Selene. I can call for a transport chopper—"

"I can walk. I just want to get out of here," she said, wrapped her arms around herself and began to rock, like a child trying to comfort itself during a nightmare.

Rhea hugged her sister and kissed her temple, trying to calm her. "It's okay, Selene. It's over. You'll be home soon."

"With you. I want to go with you," Selene cried and grabbed hold of Rhea's arm.

"With me, sis. Don't worry. You can stay as long as you need to," Rhea said.

"Let me just give my men some other instructions and then we'll head back to Regina," Jackson said.

He returned, leaving Dillon to guard Wade in the hopes he would provide more information to the CSU. They read him his Miranda rights, using Dillon's body cam to preserve it and anything else he said as evidence. He worried that if they didn't record it, it might not hold up in court, but his top priority, beside getting Selene home, was discovering if Wade and his brother had kidnapped and killed other women.

Together, Rhea and he supported Selene for the hike back to their vehicle. As they walked, she seemed to grow stronger, her back straightening and her head lifting from its earlier cowed droop. Halfway through the walk, she began her story.

"Matt and I had another fight, and he hit me again. I ran, afraid of him. Scared of myself and what I was becoming. I was driving to you, Rhea, but it was late and I got hungry. I stopped for gas and when I asked the clerk about a place to eat, he recommended the pub." She stopped to draw a shaky breath and then continued, "I ordered a burger and was eating when Earl and Wade came by. They started making comments. Eyeing me. When I left, they followed me out and catcalled me again, but I ignored them, got in my car and drove away.

"When I got to the lake, it called to me, so I parked and walked toward the shore. Stood there thinking about my life and decided it was time to leave Matt. Time to follow my dreams like you had, Rhea." She glanced at her sister and offered her a smile.

Like Rhea, Selene is even more beautiful when she smiles, Jackson thought.

"Is that when you texted me?" Rhea asked.

Selene nodded. "It is. I was going to come to you that night, but as I turned, someone grabbed me and covered my mouth. Someone else took hold of my feet to haul me back toward the road. I was kicking and trying to scream, but I couldn't breathe and passed out."

"Earl and Wade took you to the cabin?" Jackson said.

"They expected me to service them and if I didn't..." Selene's voice cracked then, and tears came to her eyes and spilled downward, but she swiped them away furiously. "They'd rape me once or twice a week. Wade really didn't want to, but Earl would bait him and say that he wasn't a real man if he didn't."

Walking beside Selene, Rhea was likewise crying, obviously thinking about everything her sister had suffered in the months she'd been held captive. The two sisters held each other, offering support. Offering comfort to each other as they finished the hike and reached the police SUVs.

Jackson helped the women into the back and got behind the wheel. It was time to return Selene to civilization. Back to her real life.

Away from Regina, he thought, but reined in his emotions. Selene was alive and free, but there might be other women who had not been so lucky.

Now it was his job to speak for them and to give their families relief. Everything else would have to wait.

Chapter Twenty-Two

Chapter Twenty-Two

Rhea had sensed his withdrawal with every mile that took them away from the cabin and to Regina. Upon their arrival, he was the consummate professional, arranging for one of the female officers to take photos of Selene and afterward getting her statement on video while he took notes. While she understood he had a job to do, it only reinforced her earlier fears that once this case was over, they'd be over.

But her pain was dimmed by the joy that Selene was alive. *Alive*, she thought and hugged her sister hard. Gazing at her, Rhea examined Selene, taking note of how she'd changed in the many months she'd been gone. There was something in her gaze that was older somehow, and there were tiny scars, the remnants of scratches and cuts, in addition to the very-visible remnants of a bruise along her cheek.

As Rhea continued her perusal, she noted additional bruising along her collarbone and bruises that looked like fingerprints on her upper arms.

Selene's gentle touch came to Rhea's jaw, urging her gaze away from the bruises. Selene was smiling, a sad smile that didn't quite reach her eyes. "I knew you wouldn't give up. I knew you'd come for me."

Rhea's gaze grew hazy with unshed tears and emotion choked her throat. She fought past it and said, "I knew you were alive. I felt it, in here." She tapped her chest.

Selene nodded. "Me, too, and I feel your pain now," she said softly and peered toward Jackson as he stood outside the interrogation room, speaking with his chief. "He's special to you, isn't he?"

Rhea closed her eyes to fight the tears and wagged her head. "He is. Very special."

"It will be all right, Rhea. Believe that," Selene said, but fell silent as Jackson returned to the room.

He laid the file in his hand on the table. It contained Selene's statement, his notes and the photos they'd taken of her various injuries. With a heavy sigh, he said, "I think we're done here, but I hope that if we need more information, you'll make yourself available."

"I will," Selene said and skipped her gaze between Jackson and her. "Do you two need a moment?"

"Yes," Rhea said at the same time that Jackson said, "No."

Rhea's heart plummeted with that, but she refused to show it. "I guess we should go now."

Jackson nodded, but didn't look at her. Instead, he focused on Selene and said, "I think you should go to the hospital."

Rhea was looking away, but she caught sight of Selene peering between them as she said, "If you think so, but what about you two—"

"Rhea wants to make sure you're safe and sound also," he replied and grabbed hold of his file. "If you don't mind, I have to head back to the cabin. The CSU team has found other victims there."

He hurried from the room, but before he did so, he gazed at her like a hungry man at a king's feast, igniting hope that he really did care. That he really wanted more for them despite his behavior.

And then he was gone to do his job, and she had her own responsibilities to fulfill. She needed to get her sister to the hospital and make sure she was fine. Once they were home, she needed to help Selene rebuild her life and get on with her own.

THE POLICE STATION still looked picture perfect, the craftsman building nestled harmoniously with the other shops along Main Street. The flowers on either side of the wide steps leading to the door had grown larger in the month since she'd last been there. As a warm breeze swept past, the petals waved at her in welcome as they had a month ago.

She only hoped she would be as welcome inside, because so much had happened in the last few weeks.

Jackson and his team had found the bodies of three other women buried a short distance from the cabin. The jewelry and other items had helped to confirm their identities. One of the women had been missing for nearly four years, and based on the date of her disappearance, as well as the others, it seemed as if the brothers had taken a new woman every year. The other victims had been taken from farther away, which was why neither the Regina nor Avalon police departments had noticed a pattern. It had kept them from being criticized in the press. If anything, Jackson and his team, as well as her, had been praised for the police work that had brought closure to the other cases and families.

Wade had confirmed that it was Earl who had been at the inn, wanting to grab Rhea so they'd have both sisters under their control. When he'd realized Rhea was no pushover, he'd decided to scare her away or kill her if need be.

Entering the building, the familiar sight of the desk sergeant was a relief. Millie would know who she was, and she suspected the other woman would know who she was there to see. She wasn't wrong, as the young police officer smiled and buzzed her through the barrier. Rising, Millie said, "It's good to see you again, Rhea. Or, at least, I hope it's a good thing."

She nodded. "It is, Millie. Wish me luck."

Millie smiled and gestured toward the back of the station. "I think you know where his office is."

"I do," she said and, without waiting, headed to see Jackson.

As she neared the door, she passed Dillon who said, "Better be careful, Rhea. He's as cross as a bear with a thorn in its paw."

Jackson's door was closed. She knocked and heard his grumbled "I'm busy" through the door.

She'd come too far to be ignored that easily. She pushed through the door and shut it behind her.

A look of surprise filled Jackson's face before he schooled his features and stood.

He took her breath away, much like he had the first time she'd seen him. His police blues seemed a little looser around his body, and his face was thinner, as well. His shortly cropped brown hair had grown out a little and the gray of his eyes was muddled, like the sky during a rainstorm. He clenched and unclenched his jaw as he stood there, clearly uneasy.

She charged on, "It's good to see you again, Jax."

"Nice to see you again, Rhea," he said, although nothing about his tone and stance said he was happy to see her.

"I know we left things on a weird note," she began, and he laughed harshly, rocked back and forth on his heels.

"That's an understatement. How is Selene? How is she doing?" he asked and relaxed a little. He invited her to sit, but she was too nervous. And too anxious about what she intended to say to him.

"She's doing well. She divorced Matt and has been seeing a therapist and going to a support group. She's also been singing at some of the local clubs."

"Sounds good." He paused, jammed his hands in his pockets and said, "How about you? You okay?"

This was the moment she'd been waiting for and she didn't hesitate to grab it with both hands. "I'm miserable. I miss you. I hated how it ended with us because… I don't want it to end, Jax. I'm in love with you."

He reared back as if he'd been struck, but then he rushed toward her and embraced her in a bear hug. "You can't imagine how many times I dreamed you'd come back and say that."

She laughed, dropped a kiss on his jaw and said, "You dreamed of me?"

"Every night, Rhea. But when we started you were so vulnerable, and I felt so guilty that I might have taken advantage. That's why I forced myself to make you leave that day. You needed space. So did I."

She playfully elbowed him and then urged him to sit with her in the chairs in front of his desk. "I was so hurt that day, but once I was back in Denver, helping Selene, I realized I needed to find out if what we had was real."

He arched a brow and took hold of her hand, lacing his fingers with hers. "And did you?"

She nodded without hesitation and squeezed his hand. "I did. I want to be with you, Jax. That is if you want to be with me."

He leaned close and laid his forehead against hers. Kissed her cheek. "I want to be with you, but your life is in Denver."

"It *was* in Denver," she said. She broke away from him only long enough to remove a key from her purse. She dangled it in front of him and, at his questioning look, she said, "I rented a storefront on Main Street for a new gallery."

"Are you sure?" Jackson asked, unable to believe that what he'd dreamed of for the last month was actually coming true. That Rhea was back. For good this time.

Rhea smiled and said, "I'm sure. I love you, Jax."

As he perused her features, her love beamed from her crystal-blue gaze, dispelling any remaining doubts he might have had.

"I love you, Rhea. I can't wait for our life together to begin."

"Why wait?" she said and pulled him up from the chair and toward the door.

Jackson laughed, but stopped at the door to kiss her. Hard. Demanding. But he tempered the kiss, worried they might not make it out of the station. As they broke apart, he cradled her face and said, "Have I ever said how much I love that you don't give up?"

"I think you called me stubborn, but that's okay, because I won't ever give up on us, Jax."

He smiled and kissed her again. "I think I can live with that. Forever, Rhea."

"Forever, Jax," she said and pulled him out the door and into the rest of their lives.

* * * * *

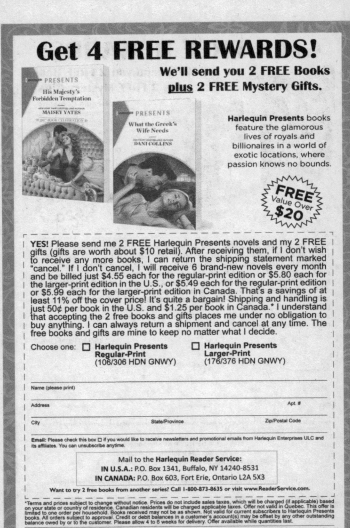

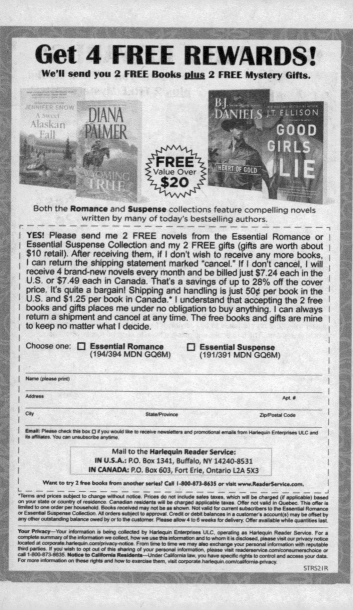

Get 4 FREE REWARDS!

We'll send you 2 FREE Books plus 2 FREE Mystery Gifts.

Both the **Romance** and **Suspense** collections feature compelling novels written by many of today's bestselling authors.

FREE Value Over **$20**

YES! Please send me 2 FREE novels from the Essential Romance or Essential Suspense Collection and my 2 FREE gifts (gifts are worth about $10 retail). After receiving them, if I don't wish to receive any more books, I can return the shipping statement marked "cancel." If I don't cancel, I will receive 4 brand-new novels every month and be billed just $7.24 each in the U.S. or $7.49 each in Canada. That's a savings of up to 28% off the cover price. It's quite a bargain! Shipping and handling is just 50¢ per book in the U.S. and $1.25 per book in Canada.* I understand that accepting the 2 free books and gifts places me under no obligation to buy anything. I can always return a shipment and cancel at any time. The free books and gifts are mine to keep no matter what I decide.

Choose one: ☐ **Essential Romance**
(194/394 MDN GQ6M)

☐ **Essential Suspense**
(191/391 MDN GQ6M)

Name (please print)

Address   Apt. #

City   State/Province   Zip/Postal Code

Email: Please check this box ☐ if you would like to receive newsletters and promotional emails from Harlequin Enterprises ULC and its affiliates. You can unsubscribe anytime.

Mail to the Harlequin Reader Service:
IN U.S.A.: P.O. Box 1341, Buffalo, NY 14240-8531
IN CANADA: P.O. Box 603, Fort Erie, Ontario L2A 5X3

Want to try 2 free books from another series! Call 1-800-873-8635 or visit www.ReaderService.com.

---

*Terms and prices subject to change without notice. Prices do not include sales taxes, which will be charged (if applicable) based on your state or country of residence. Canadian residents will be charged applicable taxes. Offer not valid in Quebec. This offer is limited to one order per household. Books received may not be as shown. Not valid for current subscribers to the Essential Romance or Essential Suspense Collection. All orders subject to approval. Credit or debit balances in a customer's account(s) may be offset by any other outstanding balance owed by or to the customer. Please allow 4 to 6 weeks for delivery. Offer available while quantities last.

Your Privacy—Your information is being collected by Harlequin Enterprises ULC, operating as Harlequin Reader Service. For a complete summary of the information we collect, how we use this information and to whom it is disclosed, please visit our privacy notice located at corporate.harlequin.com/privacy-notice. From time to time we may also exchange your personal information with reputable third parties. If you wish to opt out of this sharing of your personal information, please visit readerservice.com/consumerschoice or call 1-800-873-8635. **Notice to California Residents**—Under California law, you have specific rights to control and access your data. For more information on these rights and how to exercise them, visit corporate.harlequin.com/california-privacy.

STRS21R